BIG PICTURE

Claire Hennessy

POOLBEG

This novel is entirely a work of fiction. The names, characters and incidents portrayed in it are the work of the author's imagination. Any resemblance to actual persons, living or dead, events or localities is entirely coincidental.

Published 2008
by Poolbeg Press Ltd
123 Grange Hill, Baldoyle
Dublin 13, Ireland
E-mail: poolbeg@poolbeg.com

1 3 5 7 9 10 8 6 4 2

A catalogue record for this book is available from the British Library.

ISBN 978-1-84223-317-7

Typeset by Patricia Hope
Printed by
CPI Cox & Wyman, Reading RG1 8EX

www.poolbeg.com

About the author

Claire Hennessy lives, works, procrastinates, and writes in Dublin. *Big Picture* is her eighth book.

For more information visit *www.clairehennessy.com*.

www.clairehennessy.com

Also by Claire Hennessy

That Girl

Afterwards

Good Girls Don't

Stereotype

Being Her Sister

Memories

Dear Diary

Published by **poolbeg.com**

Acknowledgements

Writing itself is a solitary thing; babbling about writing is very much a group activity. Thank you to the friends and family who listen, support, and ask whether you're in this one – you're not, I promise, it's fiction, honestly! I adore and appreciate you all very much.

Also thanks to all at Poolbeg, for continually being wonderful, and to the readers who've enjoyed the books – you, quite simply, rock.

This one's for Paula Keatley, who is amazing in a hundred different ways.

1

Vicky

I had good intentions once upon a time. Well, September.

"Anyone get an answer for number fifteen?"

I am staring at the cover of my maths book as if it is the most fascinating thing in the entire world, as though the numbers and symbols hold the secrets of the universe. I will Ms Black not to ask me.

"Vicky?"

I look up. "I didn't get that one done," I say.

Not having your homework done for school used to be the worst thing in the world, the most dreadful offence ever. Now Ms Black just moves on, without pausing. "Laura, what did you get?"

Laura has the answer. Laura always has the answer.

I am not a fan of Laura. Laura is the teacher's pet. Laura has been the teacher's pet ever since she went and did that desperately sad and yet desperately impressive Maths Olympiad thing. Even if you don't get to the international stage, extra-curricular playing about with numbers tends to win you the eternal devotion of maths teachers.

I am only mildly jealous and not in the least bit bitter. At all.

Back in September, Ms Black told us she was going to be treating us like adults this year, which sounded like a great idea in theory. She wasn't going to come chasing after us when we hadn't done our homework. It's up to us to get it done; it's for our sake, not hers; we're the ones sitting the exams in June.

In practice what this means is that I spend every maths class hoping that she doesn't call on me for an answer, and then feeling like this when she does – totally unimportant, insignificant, not worth the energy it would take to shake a head in disappointment at the fact that I haven't done my homework.

She's been my maths teacher ever since I was a first year. Back then I was good at this stuff. Back then I understood what was going on. At some point between that and Laura being picked for the Olympiad, I stopped understanding, I guess.

I got an A in the Junior Cert, not that it means

much, really. The Leaving is different. Bigger. Harder. Back in September I thought I'd be spending every day studying, that I'd have to, that there'd be no other way around it. Sixth year. You can't just skive off in sixth year. I thought there was a part of your brain that would kick in and make that abundantly clear, so that every time you attempted to do anything that wasn't directly related to the exams, your body would reject the order and sit itself down at a desk and go over some notes or past papers or something.

I bet Laura has that in her brain. She must. Anna certainly does. Anna, who is not in this class but should be, because she's a walking talking advertisement for everything that you're supposed to do in sixth year. She studies. She knows everything that you need to know about the exam layout, the marking schemes, the timetables. She can tell you what the points are for pretty much any college course there is. I think it's highly likely that if we weren't friends, I'd be hating her an awful lot this year.

I look around the class. This is higher-level maths, a small group of us because most people have dropped down to pass over the last year or so. Anna's class is small too; they really should have just planned for the one higher-level class but they base these things on Junior Cert marks, which I think tend to give a better impression of your abilities than actually exists. Case in point that A in maths, which is a letter I haven't seen in a while now.

Everyone in this class was probably an A student once upon a time. Now we struggle. Jessica, who sits by the window and who's also in my biology class, has a question for Ms Black nearly every class. She never minds answering them; I would ask questions if only I knew what to ask. It'd be the really obvious stuff, like wondering about the basic formulas, that I'd be asking. Jessica's struggling but at least she understands enough to attempt the questions.

I think that might be the difference between me and them, all of them. I look over at the other side of the classroom. Sinéad, Sorcha, and Ruth are all getting grinds, which I used to think was a sign of being really desperate, on the verge of failure, but which seems to really be about being utterly determined to get that elusive A1.

I don't know how people find the time or the energy to put in the work that you apparently need in order to conquer the Leaving Cert maths syllabus.

Ms Black gives us four exam questions for homework. More than usual, but it's Friday. We'll have the weekend to do them.

I think wistfully of the days when Fridays meant

no homework and when weekends were supposed to be for relaxing and recuperating, guilt-free. Grown-ups are not generally expected to work over the weekend, not without being paid for it, anyway.

I reminisce about the days when I was actually smart. Or when being smart actually meant something. I'm not sure which it is.

Laura hovers after the bell goes, chatting to Ms Black about a particular question, handing over extra work she's done. The extra work sickens me, but the way Ms Black treats her like a real person, a grown-up rather than a student, doesn't in the slightest.

Back in September, when I had all my plans, I was going to ask Ms Black at some point if I could talk to her about doing maths in college, ask her what it's like. She's young enough, maybe ten years out of college if that, and infinitely more in touch with things than our guidance counsellor, who should probably retire and let Anna do her job for her. I was going to ask her and maybe then she would be all encouraging and supportive and tell me that I'd love it and that I'd be great at it and she was sure I'd get the points and all that.

Now I think she'd laugh in my face. No, not even laugh; just look confused, surprised, maybe pitying. She'd try to talk me out of it, or maybe be polite and offer advice but have no real belief in either my ability or interest. I wouldn't believe in me, if I had corrected my last three maths tests.

I mentally pull Laura's hair on my way out of the classroom. It's less satisfying than actually doing it. Life is full of disappointments.

2

Anna

It's my dad's fiftieth birthday and I haven't seen half these people since my grandfather's funeral nearly two years ago. My cousins are mostly younger – my dad is the eldest of his siblings – and at some point in the last few years, the christenings and weddings that used to mean big family get-togethers when I was younger have been replaced by funerals.

This sounds like it should be sad, but honestly there isn't much of a difference in terms of what gets talked about or how much drinking takes place. I think the sad part is that there always has to be an occasion, a strong enough motivation for people to get together.

At seventeen-going-on-eighteen I am entitled to

hang out with the grown-ups. My cousin Lily is twenty. You need to add our ages together to get the next-youngest. Charlotte, who married my dad's younger brother Phil, is thirty-seven, I think. Phil is forty-three, an older man, if six years counts at that age. Ian, the baby of the family, will be forty next year. Ian is what my dad's family refer to as 'a permanent bachelor' which is clearly a euphemism for something. It only occurred to me a couple of years ago that he might be gay, but he seems to flirt with Charlotte a lot so it's hard to tell. It is hard to tell what Phil thinks about his brother possibly flirting with his wife. He's not the talkative type and is at this very moment reading a newspaper when everyone else is swapping stories about their summer holidays. I wonder if bringing down my biology book would be more rude or on the same level.

Somehow there is a glass of wine in my hand despite the plan to stay on the Coke all night. My study plan requires getting enough sleep and not suffering the after-effects of wine consumption the next day. My study plan, apparently, does not count when it comes to things like my dad's fiftieth birthday.

I could be hiding out in my room. But that would be rude. And it's his birthday, and it's a big deal, and it's not that I don't want to be here so much as I wish

I'd been asked if I was going to be taking part in the celebrations, or something.

I suppose family commitments go unspoken. But this is November of my Leaving Cert year and the exams are in six and a half months and I haven't been out at a party since Halloween and that was mid-term break so it's different and it's like no one realises that I'm trying to take it easy, or that they think somehow family things don't leave you just as drained the morning after as going out with friends would.

The same mother who asks me how the study's going at least once a day is the one responsible for this glass of wine in my hand. I mean, honestly.

"Anna, you've exams this year, don't you?" That's Penny, my dad's sister.

I nod. "Yup."

She makes a sympathetic face. "How's it going?"

"It's okay." I don't want to say anything more than that. I don't want to talk about it. If I say that it's going well, then they'll have expectations. High hopes.

"Ah, you're brilliant, you'll be fine. Tough year, though. I think we're all still recovering from when Lily did it." She laughs.

Lily rolls her eyes.

Lily is in her third and final year of college. Four hundred and seventy points in her Leaving Cert, which I know is good and all that, and was more than she needed for Arts, but *still.*

"And Denise is doing her Junior Cert this year, which'll be another barrel of laughs, I'm sure," Penny continues. Denise is fifteen and not here tonight because apparently she can't be dragged away from her boyfriend, or so Penny says.

I remember when I was little and there'd be a christening or something on and Lily and I would run off somewhere and Denise would try to follow us, trying to be part of our grown-up talk. I always felt so mature, being on that side of the line with Lily, who I totally idolised. In my head Lily is always way older than me and Denise miles younger than us both. Now Denise is fifteen and all coupled up.

When did that happen, I wonder. When did we grow up?

"Oh, don't tell me about it," Charlotte says. "My niece – you know, Matt's little girl – she did the Junior Cert last year – he says they were more stressed about it than she was."

I hate conversations that go like this. They don't know what it's like. There is no way that my parents are ever going to be more stressed about the exams than I am. They're not the ones who have to sit them.

It's all so condescending, coming from this generation of people who still talk about how many honours someone got instead of how many A's, as though getting a C in something is worthy of admiration.

I drink my wine and say nothing. Lily tops my glass up with a knowing smile.

"You'll get through it," she says.

It is amazing how confident people can be about other people's success. Really.

Later in the evening I overhear Mom and Penny in the kitchen talking about Denise and her boyfriend.

"She's completely wrapped up in him, they're bloody inseparable, I don't know how she's going to pass her exams if she keeps this up. Studying? She doesn't know the meaning of the word. I went in to talk to her teachers the other day, she's just not working. I don't know what I'm going to do with her."

Mom says something I can't quite make out, and then something about how you're only young once.

"You're lucky," Penny says. "Anna's a good kid."

"She is."

"She's not going out with anyone, is she?"

"Not that I know of. Ah, she has her exams. I can't see her wanting to be distracted from that."

"She's very ambitious, isn't she?"

I don't hear what my mother says in response to that and I'm not sure I want to know.

3

Vicky

I answer the doorbell after the third time it rings. This is Jen's house. I shouldn't be opening the door. Jen should. She's somewhere. Upstairs, maybe. With Luke. Is Luke here yet?

"Vicky, Vicky, Vicky," Rob says, laughing as he and a couple of his friends add their coats to the pile hanging over the banister. "You're hammered. And it's not even ten yet. I'm impressed."

I make a face at him. "I am not *hammered,*" I say. "I am mildly tipsy."

He nudges me into the kitchen with the others and oh, there's Jen. She's been fashioning a beer bong. I think that's part of a garden hose she's using.

"You've always been good with your hands," Rob says to her. She sticks her tongue out at him.

Rob and Jen went out for something like two weeks once upon a time. He's one of her best friends. She has a boyfriend and he, as she has been frequently reminding me, is single. He flirts with me. Apparently. I think he flirts with everyone.

He's cute. I mean of course he's cute. He has floppy dark hair and he smiles a lot. Happy people are attractive, or something. Did Anna tell me that once? Anna knows everything.

Luke is doing a test-run with the beer and the bong and all that. I wonder if 'bonging' is an actual word. I wonder this out loud, and Chris, one of the guys who arrived with Rob, can't stop laughing at this.

They've been drinking already, I think. And Rob has the nerve to accuse me of being hammered when I am clearly not.

Okay, so I'm a little tipsy. But you know. Whatever. One is only young once. It's the weekend and all that.

I mean, I could be at home studying like a freaky Laura-type person, or I could be here watching Rob down a ridiculous amount of beer.

He's cute.

I am encouraged to have a go. I'm a part of this. I fit here. Plus this is clearly the best way to consume beer ever.

When I resume my position leaning against the counter, Rob comes and leans next to me, putting his head on my shoulder.

It feels good there, like it belongs. I smile.

4

Anna

Ambitious.

Ambition is one of those things that is always a *fatal flaw* in Shakespeare. I'm not particularly knowledgeable about Shakespeare but *Macbeth* is on our course this year, and Macbeth definitely has that fatal flaw.

You'd think Shakespeare, supposedly the greatest writer in the English language, would have been more sympathetic in dealing with ambition.

My aunt thinks I'm ambitious. Sorry, *very ambitious.* Possibly my mother agrees with her.

There is really no good way to use the word ambitious about someone, ever. It's not just about setting goals and seeing the Big Picture and working your way towards something. It's that element of ruthlessness, the implication that you would do anything to get what you want.

If you're ambitious in Shakespeare, you will kill people who are standing in your way.

And then there's the hint of presumptuousness. How dare you have such high expectations for yourself? How foolish of you. How dare you presume to think that you might achieve something? Don't you know you're not cut out for it?

I'm up in my bedroom even though there are still a handful of guests left downstairs. I open the notebook. My lists. In August, before school started, I wrote it down. The course list for the CAO, which I mean to fill out soon, even though the deadline isn't for months. Medicine, medicine, medicine. And the points you need, the points I need, last year's points plus ten or fifteen just in case. The points are supposed to be lower this year, so they say, but medicine never acts the way other courses do, and that's not going to change in time to make a difference for me. I've accepted that.

To be absolutely safe I need six hundred. Six A1s at higher level. Biology, chemistry, accounting (which I am only taking because the timetable doesn't let me do three sciences, and it is straightforward), maths (in which I am getting grinds because my teacher is absolutely hopeless and they won't let anyone move into Ms Black's class, refusing to admit that anyone on the staff might be incredibly incompetent – don't even get me started on Mrs Fitzpatrick), English, Irish. I am still in the higher-level French class but mean to drop down to pass so I can concentrate on my other subjects, the ones that I'll be counting. It just seems dangerous to do that, because what if one exam goes horribly wrong?

In the notebook there is the list of all the tests in school, all the marks I've got this year, the numerical indicators of where I am going right and where I am going wrong.

This is not ambitious. If anything it's a procrastination technique, making lists instead of studying.

I am not ambitious. I have no intention of killing anyone or bribing anyone or seducing anyone in order to get my way. Besides, they've a whole set of regulations about not sticking money inside your exam scripts, which I don't think anyone would really do, even though people joke about it all the time.

This is how it works: you work. There is no secret way around the Leaving Cert. It is not *ambitious* to understand this, or to appreciate that you can either get into the course you want this way, or wait for years and years before you can try the graduate-route or mature-student thing.

Anna's very ambitious. Please.

5

Vicky

Anna arrives within twenty minutes of my text message. This surprises me and it probably shouldn't. She lives nearby. It's not like it's a trek out to my house. It's just that lately she's been really fussy about not doing things at the last minute, not turning up to impromptu get-togethers because it interferes with her plans. Her crazy study plan.

I am trying not to think about just how much studying Anna is doing.

I'm also really really hungover, which is why I've no guilt about spending the day just watching TV and messing about online and inviting people over. It's not like I can study today anyway.

"Alan's coming over later," I tell her as she settles

into the armchair in the sitting-room, tucking her feet up underneath her.

"Oh, cool," she says.

I don't add that I invited Alan over because I suspected Anna would tell me she had too much work to do today.

"How was Jen's thing?" she asks as I make us coffee. The smell is strong and for a moment I feel nauseous, but it passes.

"Great. Rob was there."

"Ooooooh. Anything happen?"

I set her mug of coffee down in front of her and sit down with mine. "Not really." I have nothing concrete to say about it, nothing beyond the way he smiles at me or the friendliness that might be flirtation and interest but might also just be to do with drinking.

"But you think he likes you?"

"Jen thinks he does. I don't know."

"You should invite him to do something," Anna says, "just the two of you."

"Like what?"

She shrugs. "Cinema. Food. Bowling. Something."

"Bowling?" What the hell?

"It was just an example," she says. "Look, if you're always around other people, he'll be a typical boy and worried about looking cool in front of his friends.

You need to give him a chance to make a move. Or give yourself a chance to make a move."

"I think I'll just see how it goes, for the time being," I say. I am not so fond of this advice telling me to basically ask Rob out on a *date*. I mean, who goes out on dates, exactly? Dates are bizarre concepts. You don't invite someone to do something with you unless you're already together. People just – get together. It just happens.

I change the subject. "Get up to anything interesting last night?"

"Yeah, my dad's birthday, remember?"

Oh. Yes. I do remember now. Her dad just turned fifty and they were having a big family party in her house. We were even talking about it in school on Friday. I'm such a scatterbrain lately. I used to be good at remembering this stuff. I ask how it was.

"It was fine. You know. Family." She chews on her thumbnail.

"How are all the little cousins?"

"They're fine."

This is hardly riveting conversation. Maybe it's just that we're tired. Well, I'm tired. Anna looks like she is, but then again she's looked that way since September, around the same time as I lost the ability or energy to do anything with my weekends apart from go to parties and watch atrocious but addictive reality television. There's something compulsive and comforting about watching horrible people competing for jobs, starring roles, record contracts, money, whatever.

I might not have the kind of smartness that you need to do well in the Leaving, but I'm well aware that these programmes are so appealing precisely because it's not me having to compete.

There's probably something on TV now. My parents finally caved in to Tara's pestering last Christmas and got digital; which I feel wasn't the smartest move on their part, as far as thinking about the daughter who has to sit her Leaving Cert in a few months goes. But Tara is your standard baby-of-the-family sort of little sister. She's in second year, has just turned fourteen, and in general gets whatever she wants. When I was fourteen, I most certainly did not have a fancy expensive phone that takes pictures and plays music and has internet access, or get the kind of pocket money that she gets. I couldn't go out with my friends without being interrogated, or stay out late the way she does.

I also couldn't get away with getting the kind of marks she gets in school. I mean, despite the loss of whatever mathematical abilities I once had, I've still never *failed* a Christmas or a summer exam. Tara is the kind of student who worries about whether she's passed or failed, not about getting an A or a B. My parents, who once asked me tentatively if I was 'all right' when I got a C on a test, now say vague things about Tara having to work a bit harder next time when she fails something.

Because of this I am refusing to tell them anything about the marks I'm getting this year, even though they keep saying things about Tara not being 'academically inclined' and how I'm not like that. If I was 'academically inclined' this would all be easy. I would be getting A's and I'd be doing my homework and everything would be okay.

Much like the madness of having one exam determine your entire future, having a younger sister makes you very aware that fairness may be a mythical concept.

"You feel like watching this?" I ask Anna as I click my way towards a repeat of a show about models trying to survive forty-eight hours as legal secretaries. On the screen, a blonde-haired model – oh, I recognise her, she's moved on to trying to make it as a soap-opera actress – is cracking up because the pressure is just too much.

"Ick. No. Turn it off."

"But it's funny!"

"It's *crap*. Life is too short for bad television."

The latter comment dispels my urge to throw

something at her for being a snob. I snort. "You're ridiculous."

She considers this. "That's quite possible."

And then Alan's at the door, arriving just in time to be curious about why we're laughing. If I had to analyse it, I would classify it as half-hysterical laughter, the combination of sixth-year stress and the way it's just a little bit harder these days for us to find something to talk about. I don't want to rip the Rob thing to shreds just yet, and she – I don't even know what she's up to, if there's anything beyond the manic studying. She won't come to most of the parties, even though she's invited; Jen and everyone are her friends as much as they are mine.

It's like she's looking down on all that in some way, like she's so much better than drinking and hanging out and the boys like Rob. Possibly that's why I don't want to dissect the situation with her. And it's not like I don't want to be friends with her anymore. It's not like that. I'm not sure what it's like but it's not that.

Anna and I have been friends ever since first year, when we had to get into groups for something in business studies class, I can't even remember what it was now. We had a young hippie-ish teacher that year; I think now it must have been her first year teaching. She wore a lot of flowing skirts and spoke earnestly about the importance of teamwork and co-operation and respecting one another. She left at the end of the year, maybe realising that such ideals had no place in either business studies or the Irish educational system. But she was absolutely obsessed with group stuff, and Anna and I were stuck with two completely brainless idiots who spent every class either whispering or else playing around with their phones.

It is a well-known fact that nothing makes people bond quite as rapidly as the mocking of others. Behind their backs, obviously, because brainless idiots have a tendency to be the same people who have a large group of friends well-acquainted with the ins and outs of intimidation. One of those girls later got expelled – well, not technically *expelled* but not-so-nicely asked not to return the following year – for bullying. The other is better at avoiding getting caught.

At any rate we ended up being friends, and hanging out with some of the other girls in our year. Lisa's gone now, having decided that a cram school was the only way to go for sixth year. Sinéad stopped being friends with us for a while and went through a weird stage, but she's friends with Jen now, who only came to the school last year, so I guess we're friends again, or friendly, anyway. Emma abandoned all of her friends for the sake of her completely disgusting, horrible boyfriend a while back so she's basically out of the picture. She's not in any of my classes anymore anyway.

Anna and I have always agreed on the vileness of Emma's boyfriend, theorised about Sinéad's oddness, and rolled our eyes at Lisa's misguided ideas about having the secrets of the Leaving Cert unveiled just because she's paying three times as much for her education this year. It's not like we agree about everything, but she's always been the person I could count on to understand my thoughts about something, whether it's the bizarre attitudes of boys or the fact that 84% is a mark to be disappointed by rather than proud of. (Plus it's just *cruel*, so painfully close to an A but still not there.)

At some point I have been forced to stop thinking that I can afford to turn my nose up at any mark in the 80s, and Anna has chosen to live in the world of theoretical information rather than the real one, and just doesn't understand what's going on with me and Rob or how people actually interact.

But when we're giddily saying "Oh, nothing" to Alan, as he looks bemusedly at us both, everything feels like it's all right, for the moment.

6

Anna

I'm over at Vicky's house because the wine from last night is still somewhere in my system, tapping at the inside of my skull and reminding me that one must pay the price for alcohol consumption. As though I didn't know that already. There's no way I'll get anything substantial done today, and that bothers me; it's so easy to get into the habit of not doing any work and putting things off and then before you know it the exams are happening and you're completely unprepared. I keep thinking of Rip Van Winkle and the way he woke up after all those years. I wonder if that could happen with this year, if you could just fall asleep now and then wake up in June on the day of your first exam. It's a terrifying prospect.

And Alan's here, which is another reminder. What happens when you choose parties over studying.

"Out last night?" Vicky asks him.

"Yeah, James had a few of us over," he says, and launches into a tale of drunken silliness. I quickly lose track of the names. James is the only one of Alan's friends I know, as in have spoken to more than once, and that's only because he's giving me maths grinds. James isn't much older than us – he's in his second year of college, doing maths, obviously – so the whole thing was a little weird at first. It was Vicky's idea ("Oh, you know, James gives grinds, you should talk to him, he'd be great") and I was initially reluctant, but decided to give it a try. I think we knew each other just well enough to be able to casually chat but not so well that him being the one in charge was strange.

James is quite simply brilliant. I also happen to think he's very attractive but it's the sort of thing that will always be a hopeless crush.

James and Alan went to school together. Alan was always really involved in extra-curricular activities – he knows Vicky from her debating days. James was less involved but not completely reclusive either; they were both expected to do very well in their exams but maybe not exceptionally well, as I understand it.

James's uncle died suddenly in the middle of the

exams. James sat the rest of them but after having something like that happen had a lot of 'perspective' on the matter and at the end of the day they were only exams. So when they got their results at the end of the summer, Alan wasn't expecting his friend to do really well. Exceptionally well. Five hundred and seventy points kind of well. Alan got five hundred, not enough for any of his top choices, not what he had been hoping for, and ended up in his seventh preference, something to do with finance, which he'd put down half-heartedly just to fill space. He dropped out after two months, worked for the rest of the year, and is now repeating. His attitude is that the time out and the experience in the 'real world' have left him in a much better position to tackle the exams this time around.

I like Alan, and I think he's quite clever, but I'm convinced this is some kind of defence mechanism. Working in a minimum-wage job for several months can't possibly be all that life-changing, and honestly that 'real world' idea bothers me, as though exams aren't the 'real world', as though working hard towards a particular goal is something that one will never have to do in this so-called 'real world'. If I was repeating the Leaving – oh, I don't even want to contemplate that idea – it would *kill* me if my friends were already in their second year of college.

Plus, what on earth is he doing, having all these

crazy drunken escapades – the part of the story he's telling now involves six of them squeezing into a telephone booth and then getting stuck – when he should be studying, i.e. doing what he *didn't* do the last time around?

From what I've read it is generally not advisable to repeat the Leaving Cert unless there are extenuating circumstances, like you've been sick or there's some really big reason why you didn't do your best. Apparently if you do well – this is said by people who view five hundred points as doing 'well', regardless of whether you've got into the course you want or not – you're not likely to improve all that much on your second try.

These are the things that I read about when my time could be much more productively used to actually learn the things I need to learn in order to not end up in the situation where I would need to consider whether or not to repeat. I bite my nails and decide that when I get home I'll get *something* done.

I need to stop biting my nails. They look horrible. I'll give it up next summer.

"Anna? You with us?" Vicky's waving at me.

"What? Oh, sorry. I was just thinking." I hate the way headaches disrupt concentration.

"About anything interesting?" Alan wants to know.

I shrug. "Not really."

"No men on the horizon?" he asks.

"Nope," I say, and that's the end of that. I feel both incredibly boring and irritated. What is this constant obsession with people's love lives all about? Why is it a topic that comes up again and again and again? Every day in school we wind up talking about someone's love life, someone's romantic saga. Jen and her boyfriend Luke and whether or not they can sustain their relationship, a debate that was interesting the first time around and less so the tenth. She's not sure she wants to stay with him, but always, always decides not to rock the boat. Sinéad and the constant stream of guys in her life, a new soul-mate every month. Vicky and Rob and the will-they-won't-they dance that they've apparently been doing for the past couple of weeks, flirting at parties but not saying outright that they're interested in one another. I'm not particularly impressed with Rob, to be quite honest; there isn't anything special about him from what I can see. He's charming and fun and I suppose good to socialise with on a superficial level, but I can easily imagine that ten years from now he won't have changed much. He'll still be telling the same stories and behaving the same way towards girls and will be more concerned with having fun than actually doing something with his life.

Vicky, I have always thought, is far too smart to get involved with someone like Rob. She's not like our (now former) friend Emma, who threw everything in her life away for the sake of her boyfriend. Emma and Paul are planning to spend the rest of their lives together, never mind the fact that he's jealous, controlling and manipulative. Never mind that she used to be friends with us and used to do well in school, and now comes in late all the time and has teachers asking her to stay after class to discuss her work. She actually fell asleep in French the other day. Right in the middle of class. Unbelievable. And it's not as though you can *talk* to her. When she's not falling asleep, her eyes are glued to the screen of her mobile phone, reading what I presume are appropriately devoted text messages from her beloved Paul. I remember when she used to have a personality of her own.

That is what relationships do to people. I think about Denise and how even two years ago she wouldn't have passed up a chance to be among the 'older' cousins at a family gathering for anything. Why everyone seems to think as though you are somehow less of a person if you're not involved with someone is completely baffling. If anything the reverse is true.

It makes you feel as though you're inadequate, not

to have someone. Oh, no men in your life? Clearly you have nothing else interesting to say. Let's move on.

I listen to Vicky and Alan talk and I know that I don't have anything interesting to say. It's hard to be indignant about something when you know it's not entirely inaccurate.

7

Vicky

Anna says she needs to be home in time for dinner, which sounds like an excuse but I let it slide. I hug her goodbye and Alan does a nod-and-wave combination. The second she's gone, I turn to Alan and ask him whether he has a thing for her.

"For Anna?"

"Yeah. Asking her about her love life, what's that all about?"

"It's called making polite conversation," he says, looking serious rather than embarrassed about it. Either he really isn't interested in her or his time in the workforce has left him a much more mature, sensible boy. He's nineteen. I suppose we're past the immature teenager stage, or should be.

I look at him and wonder if he thinks I'm so terribly immature, seeing romance everywhere. For a moment I think he does, and I feel very young, so very clearly on the other side of the 'adult' line.

"Anyway, aren't we supposed to be waiting for her and James to get together?" he grins, and I feel better.

"Yeah. Has James said anything to you about her?"

Alan shrugs. "Nothing much. But he was complaining about the lack of women in his class."

"He actually said 'women'? When do we become *women*?"

"Apparently when you go and study maths in college and James says you're one," Alan says, and we laugh. "You're still putting that down, right?"

"Putting what down?" I ask, attempting to sound vague.

"Maths, Vicky." Alan has known me since I was fourteen and still thinks I'm actually good at that stuff. "What courses have you looked at?"

I shrug. "I don't know."

"Vicky."

"I don't *know*, okay? I don't have to decide right away what I want to do."

"Well, what are you thinking about doing?" He's persistent.

I am thinking about doing something which

doesn't require me to get a high grade in Leaving Cert maths, for a start. I'm thinking about something which won't make me feel like crap. I'm thinking about being finished with school and not having to deal with this kind of intense once-off one-chance all-or-nothing two-years-of-work-in-three-weeks exam situation.

What courses have I looked at? Every maths-related course you can apply for via the CAO. Mathematical science. Physics, computers, engineering, economics. Maths as part of an arts degree and as part of a science degree. I haven't found the perfect course yet, not like Anna and her medicine, and every time I read over the information I have, or think about it, it seems a little less like something I might want to do. I don't know what else I want to do. I just know that I'm tired of this, all of this.

"Arts. Science. Something," I say finally. Something that doesn't put me into a little box before I even get to college. Some umbrella course that lets you make your decisions after the Leaving Cert and not before it. Something which doesn't require high points. Something I can think about at a later date.

"Vicky."

"We're not all as focussed as you, okay? Stop being so pushy," I say, meaning it to be light. It's not.

"I wasn't," he says coldly.

"Yeah, you were." I hate it when people claim not to have been doing something when it's so blatantly obvious that they were. *Hate* it. I'm not an idiot. I can't be fooled into thinking something other than the truth simply because someone speaks in that horrible I-know-better-than-you tone. Tone sometimes works as a tactic, but if you don't have the evidence to back you up, you fall flat on your face. If we were arguing this in front of an audience he'd know not to make that mistake.

"Fine. Go ahead. Fuck things up for yourself. Good luck with that." And he's out the door before I can think of anything coherent to say in response to that. Another great tactic – leave before what you say has the chance to be attacked for being so completely ridiculous and *stupid*.

I can't believe he genuinely thinks that the world's about to end just because I don't know for sure what I'm going to do in college. You'd think someone who managed to step off the academic treadmill for the best part of a year would have a little bit more perspective.

Look, I know I want to go to college. That much I know. I don't want to spend time stacking shelves or making coffee or doing any of the other things Alan did after he dropped out. I'm just not excited about it. I'm not *anything* about it right now.

It's a really nice idea, college. Learning about something that you're really interested in for three or four years and then getting a degree at the end of it. The trouble is that to get there you have to go through all this crap. You have to do these exams, and you have to work for these exams, and then you find that you just *can't,* and even though you're supposed to be the smart one in the family, you realise that it's over. Being smart. It's over.

You can't fuck things up for yourself if that's just how things are. And that *is* just how things are. I'm not driven or focussed or brilliant. I'm just not. It's not that I don't want to be any of those things, but that I can't be.

I sit down in front of the computer, because even though the hangover's not quite as bad as it was this morning, there's no way I can study now, and pointedly ignore the bookmarked college sites in favour of one of the online forums I've been hovering in since September. There's been a discussion raging over the merits of reality television for the last couple of days and amidst the bad spelling there are some really good points being made.

I post a response, and keep the window open while I check on my profiles on various 'social networking' sites, which is an interesting grown-up euphemism for any website that facilitates obsessing over people when you should be doing something more productive with your time. Case in point: I could right now be doing my maths homework (well, no, I couldn't, because the questions are impossible, but you know what I mean) or I could be seeing if Rob has left me a comment. Or if anyone has left him a comment since last night, ideally one that includes some reference to whether or not he might be interested in me. Or if anyone has put up photos that perhaps include him. Or – well, whatever. Something.

There's nothing interesting, really. A comment left by a very pretty girl who sounds very friendly but turns out to be his cousin, so that's all right. I reply to the new posts in the TV debate. I check my email.

It's nearly midnight before I realise it, and closer to one by the time I turn off the computer. I'm not sure where the time goes, or how the year is moving along both too slowly and too quickly. That has to go against the laws of physics. I think about time travel and all the waffly temporal concepts *Star Trek* has come up with that have no basis in fact whatsoever. I've just about concocted an explanation for this contradictory temporal flow – one that would be plausible in sci-fi, if not in a lab – when I slide off into the land of dreams.

8

Anna

He's looking at me like I'm an idiot. I consider, not for the first time, if this is what I really want to spend my Tuesday evenings doing.

"I just don't know when you've proven something," I say, fighting the redness in my cheeks. "I mean, I think I know how to do it, sort of, but I don't know at what point you've really *proven* it. If that makes sense."

"Okay," he nods, looking thoughtful. "Let me see what you have there."

I pass the sheets over to him, pages and pages of past paper questions. Maths paper two will be my downfall, I can feel it.

He looks at the question, glances at the marking

scheme for a second, and crosses off half of what I have, then adds another couple of lines, finishing with a confident Q.E.D.

I look over it. Ah. Right. That's what I need to do. That makes sense. I think. Unless my understanding of mathematical concepts is at a completely different level and the way James thinks about these things is far deeper and profound. Which is quite possible.

"How's that?" he asks.

"Perfect," I say, and we move on to the next question.

In theory, finding James attractive is a positive thing. It is productive. It means that I don't call him to cancel our sessions even if I'm sick or in that PMS-related stage where everything in the world makes me want to burst into tears. This is partly because calling would mean talking to him over the phone, a terrifying prospect, and partly because cancelling would mean not seeing him, and I do like seeing him, even if I have trouble breathing in the hour or so before he's due to arrive.

We have these sessions in the spare room upstairs that we use both for guests and for studying. My mom went back to college a few years ago to get a degree in history, and my dad is currently working his way through a part-time arts degree. I suppose you could see me as the classic case of the girl who's expected to live out the dreams her parents were never able to fulfil, but I don't think that's true. Dad will have his degree before I have mine. You don't need to get your daughter to live out your ambitions if you've already succeeded. And neither of them have any interest in medicine, apart from watching medical dramas. We are working our way through the *ER* DVDs at the moment, one or two episodes a week. I point out the medical inaccuracies, my mom notes anything the characters say about themselves that seems to contradict something that happens in a later episode, and my dad ponders on the philosophical questions that are apparently being raised. They're hardly pushing me into the field of medicine the way that parents of 'smart' kids apparently do all the time, if you believe what people say about the numbers sticking medicine down on their CAO forms.

This room has a fold-out bed that is currently in its sofa guise, and underneath and next to the desk are piles of books that could easily distract someone from studying maths. It's all my dad's stuff, books on philosophy and literary theory and the history of music, subjects that I am not usually interested in but might find fascinating if it meant I didn't have to fiddle about with formulae and Greek letters and square roots and circles.

It would be very easy to be diverted, were it not

for the fact that, when James is in the room, my attention doesn't wander. It is entirely focussed on him. This is why this arrangement is a positive and productive one. In theory.

As it turns out, being focussed on James doesn't necessarily mean being focussed on what he's saying, so much as the way he's saying it and the way his voice sounds to my ear.

There are certain things you expect from someone as brilliant as James. You expect that he will be obviously nerdy, with too-short trousers that went out of style twenty years ago and oversized glasses that keep sliding down his nose. You expect a high squeaky voice and a sense that even at almost twenty he is a twelve-year-old boy.

What you don't expect: that the cliché about glasses making people look smarter is actually true in some cases, and that smart is, in fact, sexy. That James dresses well, today sporting a pair of ripped jeans that are neither too short nor unfashionable, indicating an awareness of but not a slavish adherence to what is appropriate attire for a young man these days. That the artful tear at his knee makes me think of children with wobbly lower lips who've fallen on gravel and scraped their knee and need it made better with a kiss. That when he speaks about maths – which is quite different from when he's being conversational –

he is earnest and passionate and entirely unashamed of this.

The actual content of his speech is something that I do try to pay attention to, because it's why we're here and why my parents leave money for him in a discreet envelope on the kitchen table every week. Mostly I manage. It's just that sometimes the little things send my mind elsewhere. Like his hair, which is dark blonde and curls slightly, and which somehow balances on the tightrope between girlishly long and unpleasantly short. I'm not quite sure how he does it. If you start thinking about the magical qualities of his hair – well, that's the evening gone. You start wondering about whether he spends hours in front of the mirror every day, only he couldn't possibly, because he's not that sort of guy – except maybe he is and I just don't know him well enough to determine that, or maybe he's secretly desperately insecure about his appearance but would never admit it, which is a thought that tugs at my insides and makes me wish I had any kind of artistic skills so that I could reveal his own beauty to him via the medium of painting or something. Foolish ideas, stupid ideas. His hair does not seem overly tampered-with. So then you start thinking about genetics and wonder what kind of hair his parents and grandparents have, wonder about his entire family.

You start imagining a situation in the future when you're a doctor and he's a patient suffering from some as-yet-undiagnosed but not life-threatening illness and your examination of him involves an extensive inspection of his hair, using the very unscientific methods of running your fingers through it and looking into his eyes only to find that he's gazing adoringly at you. And then it quickly slips into the sort of thing that you really shouldn't be thinking about when you're supposed to be doing – what are we doing now? Geometry? Are we still there?

"Does that make sense?" he asks, and I am left with no alternative but to meekly ask if he could perhaps run through it one more time, just to make sure. If I were paying less attention I might not pick up on the hint of exasperation as he explains again. Just a hint, not enough to legitimately criticise him for, but there all the same, detectable only to the hyper-aware. I bite the nail on my left ring finger.

"Okay," I say when he's finished. "I think I get it."

He grins. "Cool. Okay. I think we're due for a break, don't you think?"

"Yeah," I nod, and try not to think about various fantasies in which taking a break would mean utilising that sofa-bed.

The times when I do understand what he's saying

are what make it worth it. The way that he smiles, the nod of approval, the recognition that I'm not really quite as idiotic I might seem to be sometimes. I have no interest in being the ditzy one, the girl who's cute and sweet and who boys like but don't respect. I can't imagine being the pretty kind of girl. I'd rather be smart.

I want James to think that I am smart, which is an impossibility for now, when I'm struggling with Leaving Cert maths and he's doing a degree in the subject. There's an unavoidable inequality there. Maybe in a few years, when we're grown-ups. I mean, he's already a grown-up, I suppose, and I'm close enough, technically, but I mean when we have careers. When he's – whatever maths graduates go on to do, and when I'm a doctor, when I've finished with my ten million years of training (all right, that's an exaggeration, but not by much), then maybe there could be something. Maybe.

Right now I'm just the silly little schoolgirl with a goal that I may or may not be able to achieve. I'm trying not to think about what to do if I don't get into medicine. The graduate-entry route means having to kill time, having to study something that I'm not passionate about and do reasonably well at it in order to finally get to do what I want. I've spent enough time having to jump through hoops and fulfil requirements. English, for God's sake. It's a two-paper exam testing my ability to babble on about poetry and plays, which is neither a crucial life skill nor useful for my future studies. Irish, a dying language taught badly, the most ridiculous compulsory subject ever. I just want to jump ahead to the future, to next autumn, when all this is over and I'm on the road I need to be on. When I'm out of school and the land where people study because they have to, and in a world where people study because they want to.

I think part of why I find James so appealing is because he's in that world. I like the idea of being attracted to someone simply because of what they represent; it seems like the sort of thing that will work very well as a motivator. If I have to have a crush on someone this year he'll do. It's better than liking someone like Rob, who I can't imagine serving as an inspiration for anything remotely useful.

I watch him checking his phone, the way his fingers move over the keys. I appreciate the beauty of it quietly, which is completely allowed. This is a break, it doesn't count as being distracted.

9

Vicky

It's sort of scary how school works in sixth year. Because, sure, you have the teachers who tell you that you need to work really hard and all that, but then you have the ones who remind you to get plenty of sleep and exercise and do all those things that well-rounded individuals do. And then there's all the stuff that sixth years are supposed to organise, like activities for the younger students (mostly it's the prefects, the Chosen Few who were nuts enough to accept responsibility for looking out for a particular class, who sort this stuff out, but the rest of us get dragged into it every so often) or our own special sixth-year things. We are currently having a meeting about our pre-Debs, which is in December. The organising committee want to address the entire year.

I do find myself wondering why the process of booking somewhere for a night involves an entire committee, and also how those organising-types find the time to do anything else. I mean, I used to be the sort of girl who'd get involved in things. Debating, the recycling committee, helping to organise fund-raisers. I figured that this year I wouldn't have time for that, I'd be working so hard. Which I'm not, obviously, but I don't think I'd like to have any of those kinds of commitments right now. They involve effort, and doing things like standing up in front of people and being falsely enthusiastic, like Natalie's being right now.

"It's going to be a really great night and we hope that you're all going to have a really great time," she says, pushing her hair behind her ears.

Natalie is an energetic public speaker but not a terribly interesting one. I have mostly dealt with her in the past through fund-raising stuff. She was a debater very briefly. It doesn't suit her. Debating involves having to be mean to people, even if it's only for the duration of a particular argument. With committees, with organising things, you need to try to please everyone. It suits people who want everyone to like them.

I decide, right now, that she is annoying and fake and that I never want to be one of those people, those super-active, super-involved, super-energetic types. I don't think I could be. Having to smile that much would wear me out.

"That was so pointless," Anna says when it's over. "Did we really need a whole meeting to go over all the stuff that we already knew?"

"Apparently we did," Jen yawns. "What time is it?"

I push up the sleeve of my school blouse to check my watch, but the bell gets there before me. Lunch. Excellent.

In what the school have optimistically labelled the 'restaurant', we sit at our usual spot and Anna picks up where she left off in her anti-meeting speech.

"It's such a stupid idea, anyway," she says. "A pre-Debs. We don't have our Debs until, when, this time next year? It's just an excuse for the whole year to go out drinking, and you know what? I'm not sure I want to go drinking with most of these people."

"Hear hear," Sinéad says.

Jen hasn't had quite as much time to develop an antipathy towards people as the rest of us have. "I don't know, I think it's going to be fun," she says.

"I think it's going to be *really great,*" Anna giggles, imitating Natalie's hand-clasping gestures. "Thank you all *so* much for making the effort to come today, even though we didn't *really* give you any choice."

Natalie passes by just at the wrong moment, having heard enough to stop right next to our table and say huffily, "I really don't appreciate that, Anna."

Sinéad rolls her eyes at this little scene, a gesture which seems to infuriate Natalie even more.

"You know what?" she says coldly, to all of us now. "I don't know what your problem is, but I think it's really immature to act like that around people who are actually making an effort and *doing* something for our year."

Jen, Sinéad and Anna are apparently silenced by this. Natalie smirks self-righteously.

"Oh, for God's sake," I say, exasperated. "Natalie, you just held a twenty-minute meeting to relay information that, a) everyone already knew and b) should've taken five minutes at most to get through. You then have the *nerve* to come over here and try to take up even more of our time by eavesdropping on a private conversation we were having and *insisting* on getting involved. And as if that wasn't bad enough, you've just insulted all of us by saying that we're immature, which is the sort of word that always reveals more about the person using it than the people it's directed towards. So if you don't *mind*, I think we'd all be better off if you'd kindly get lost."

And she does. I'm not the getting-involved type

anymore, I don't need to be nice to her. And God, that felt so good.

We all burst out laughing as soon as she's gone.

"You are my hero," Jen says.

"I think that might be one of those sixth-year moments I will cherish forever," Anna muses.

"I know! So this is what they mean when they talk about the best days of your life," Sinéad laughs.

Natalie storms back to us before the end of lunch, informing us coldly that she hopes we're not expecting to be able to get tickets to the pre-Debs.

"Excuse me?" Jen says.

"I just don't think you'd really enjoy the night," she says smugly. "It's not really your sort of thing, is it?" And she saunters off again, before any of us have a chance to respond.

"She can't do that," I say. "There's no way she can get away with it." I firmly believe this. One word to any of the teachers about someone trying to exclude anyone from an event and it'd put an end to allowing any of this organisational stuff to happen within school hours. The others seem less convinced.

"I don't know," Sinéad says.

Anna shrugs. "Does it matter?"

"Yeah," I say, as though it's a given, and then I think about it. "It's not fair to tell us we *can't* go, to not even give us the choice."

"It's *really* not fair," Jen says, and now I feel a little guilty for not just letting Natalie's remarks slide.

"She's just doing this because you made her look stupid," Anna says. "Which she *deserved.* Come on, let's just not go. Do we really want to be around people like that all night?"

The unanimous answer to that is no, but it's the principle of the thing. Still, none of us particularly want to confront Natalie (well, I'm half-tempted, but I suppose that's just looking for trouble) or go telling on her like a five-year-old.

"Let's just do something else that night," Jen suggests. "Get dressed up, go out somewhere nice . . ." She looks around hopefully.

"Like an anti-pre-Debs," Anna says.

"Yes. Exactly. Come on, it'll be fun!"

I find myself in favour of this idea, as long as we don't actually have to call it an anti-pre-Debs. That would just be ridiculous, two steps away from living in an American teen drama series and having an Alterna-Prom. We settle on calling it an Excuse Party, as in Excuse To Dress Up And Drink.

"Me and Vicky will organise it," Jen says.

"I don't remember agreeing to that," I laugh.

"Come on, you know you want to. It's not like we can get these two to do anything," she says, nodding towards Anna and Sinéad.

"Excuse me?" Sinéad says.

"No, no, that's fair enough," Anna says, smiling. "I don't want to be on your *committee*, anyway."

"Hey. We're not going to have a committee," Jen says. Then she considers this. "Oh, but we could! With a *chairperson!* I could be a chairperson!"

The scary thing is that she's only half-joking. "I think we'll manage," I say.

"We. Aha. Knew I could count on you."

And that is how I somehow end up doing exactly what I was planning to avoid, in a position of sort-of responsibility, with a commitment involving effort that will only further distance me from all the studying I really should be doing. I'm an idiot, clearly.

And yet there is a part of my brain already compiling a list of possible venues. If only this was the sort of stuff they tested you on in the Leaving.

10

Anna

Little-known fact: I was planning on avoiding the pre-Debs entirely. The whole concept is just so absurd. It's such a middle-class, nothing-better-to-do-with-our-time, privileged-little-daddy's-girls thing to have. It's the sort of event that people organise because they have foolish ideas about how well everyone gets along and how it's oh-so-important for the entire year to spend time together, as though we haven't all been stuck together for six years. It's an excuse to buy a dress that isn't quite as expensive as your Debs dress will be but is getting there, to wear uncomfortable shoes, and to agonise over the issue of who to bring with you.

It was so easy objecting to the pre-Debs. It's

organised by irritating people who seriously think that your time at school counts as the 'best days of your life'. Who in their right mind wants to spend an entire night hanging around with those kinds of people?

But now we have our alternative. Vicky and Jen are organising an Excuse Party for the same night, which is completely up-front about the fact that it's really all about the alcohol and the fancy clothes, and that's something that's harder to argue against. They're both really excited about it. Jen's persuaded several of the non-irritating types at school to come along – Natalie, one of the pre-Debs organisers, is absolutely fuming – and Vicky's been in Project Mode this past week or so, permanently attached to her To Do lists. She has somehow, miraculously, sorted out a not-unpleasant venue that was still taking bookings for December; it's local rather than in the city centre but apparently that's not a problem as we'll be there for the night anyway (what is this fascination people have with starting off in one place and then moving on? Why not just go to the place you want to go to first off? I don't get it) and they're more lenient about IDs anyway.

I have not commented on the fact that this is so clearly a procrastination technique on Vicky's part, because, well, she must know that it is. And honestly

I think Vicky's going to be fine anyway. Vicky is the kind of student that I think well-meaning but clueless relatives assume I am – naturally brilliant. When we were sitting the Junior Cert – you know, that exam that seems really stressful at the time until you realise that it doesn't actually count towards anything – she left every single exam early. Which I suppose you can get away with when it's the Junior Cert – I did leave a couple before the time was up – but, honestly, every single exam. Compulsive early leavers tend to be either outstanding or abysmal. It takes either a lot of confidence or a lot of apathy to be able to walk out early on your one opportunity to sit a paper.

I double- and triple- and quadruple-checked everything I put down on the page, usually refusing to leave before the exam was officially over because I just *couldn't.* Leaving early is asking for trouble; the second you hand over your script, some detail you've left out or messed up will strike you with the force of lightning and you'll be left absolutely powerless to do anything about it. Why risk it?

So I did things my way and Vicky did things hers, and we both ended up with a string of A's with a lone B (mine was in French, hers was in Business Studies). Respectable results that make you feel smart for about a fortnight and that are entirely, depressingly meaningless in the long run. At the time, you're thrilled with yourself, of course, because you're young and completely lacking in perspective. You don't realise that you'll have to do the same thing all over again a few years later, only it'll be harder and it will mean more. It will mean everything.

I think that someone who was able to leave every single exam early and still come out with those results is in a far better position to face these exams than someone like me. I mean, of course you have to do the work. But you do sort of wonder, sometimes, at what point that just isn't enough.

I want to believe that it's enough to work and to be reasonably intelligent and that you don't need to be absolutely brilliant.

And then I think about Vicky. And Alan and James, and how that worked out. And how I need – want – *need* – my six A1s, my six hundred points, and how that seems like the most impossible thing in the world sometimes and I don't understand how *anyone* can achieve that unless they're total geniuses. I can't even bear to think about the stories that run in the newspapers every summer, the students with their eight or nine A1s, holding up their results sheet with a self-satisfied smirk on their faces and usually claiming to be well-rounded individuals on top of it all. I don't understand how those people can exist.

But Vicky – Vicky does not need anyone worrying

about her. Vicky will be fine. Vicky will organise this Excuse Party that I, perhaps appropriately enough, can't find an excuse to avoid, and I will be awkward and hopeless and dateless.

In my fantasies, which are interrupting the English essay I'm supposed to be devoting my evening to, James keeps on asking me about this Excuse Party which he says wistfully sounds sort of cool, until finally I suggest that he comes along, and his face lights up.

And that's absolutely ridiculous. James may be still living at home but he's a *college student*. He's past this era of sixth-year get-togethers. There is no way on earth that he would ever be remotely wistful about something that a bunch of schoolgirls were organising. That's the trouble with fantasies. They lack plausibility.

I am sitting at my desk – the one in my bedroom rather than the spare room, the one that I won't let James near because that would just be too much for me – and tapping my pen against the page.

He's such a distraction. Why is it that all those 'how to study' advice things never include nuggets like 'avoid developing crushes on anyone, particularly someone you see on a weekly basis'? Of course, maybe I only find him attractive because he's there, and because I *need* a distraction, an excuse not to study. That seems like a reasonable hypothesis, right?

Right, doctor, you've made your diagnosis, I say to

myself. What next? What's the cure for infatuation?

I sigh and abandon the essay for the duration of exactly one episode of *Scrubs* (on DVD, which means no ads, which means efficient television-watching). If I were planning to become a TV-doctor having an overactive imagination would not be a problem. That is what I learn from my twenty-three minute break. Unfortunately this doesn't really help with trying to write about the poetry of Seamus Heaney.

I am on the second line of my first paragraph and I can't think of what I want to say. God, this is so ridiculous. It's one of those waffly questions about what feelings the poems inspire in you and why you would recommend that teenagers read Heaney's work, one of those stupidly worded questions where they're trying to soften the blow by couching it all in personal terms. What do you like, what do you think. They are not in the least bit interested in what you think, really. They just want to know that you can write several pages about themes and imagery and symbolism and all that nonsense. The feelings that these poems inspire in me include bafflement and boredom. No examiner wants to read about that.

I remind myself that it is nearly December, and that English is the first exam in June, and that means there's only six and a bit months until I never ever have to do any of this stuff ever again.

I stare at the page again and make a deal with myself. Get to the end of the first paragraph, and then I can take another break. What actually happens is that once I get into it, I don't look up until the thing's written, which is what I was quietly hoping for in the first place, at the back of my mind.

I cross the essay off my list for this week and grin.

To Do List: Vicky

Double-check w/ Tiger Bar re: reservation
Homework
Find dress
Haircut?
Call Alan re: open day (& party?)
Check w/ Jen re: Rob
'Make or Break' (new series back on Thurs)
Shoes!

To Do List: Anna

Homework:
Maths (for J).
Maths (for school).
Accounting (2003 Q5).
Irish (poetry Qs).

Reading:
English ('Dancing At Lughnasa', Act I).
Chemistry (revision book, chapter 4).

Notes:
Biology (chapters 13-14).
Chemistry (chapters 24-26).

Other:
Email Lily back.
Open day (Wednesday).
Christmas shopping (Wednesday).
Excuse Party (Saturday).

11

Vicky

Alan's been ignoring my text messages for the past fortnight and refuses to have a profile on any site which one could leave comments on ("I am not turning into one of those people who conduct their social lives online, Vicky"), so I end up calling him. "Are you still pissed off with me?" I ask.

"Who's calling?"

"What do you mean, who's calling? My number always comes up on your phone."

He pauses, and then says, "Hi, Vicky. How are you doing?"

"I'm fine. And you're ignoring me."

"I'm not ignoring you. I've just been busy. Studying. You know how us *focussed* people are."

"You *are* focussed. And I'm jealous, you *know* I'm just jealous."

"What do you mean you're jealous?"

I hate having to explain it. He should know what I mean. "I wish I was focussed. I would *love* to be focussed. I just don't have that gene, or whatever it is."

He laughs. "Vicky, you know that's total crap, right?"

"Excuse me?"

"There's no gene for it," he says. "Ask Anna, she'll back me up."

"I was being metaphorical," I reply, slightly indignant at this point. Of course I know there's not an actual focussed *gene*. It's a figure of speech to convey the way in which some people are more naturally suited than the rest of us to the maniacal studying patterns the Leaving Cert requires.

"Okay, okay. What's up, anyway?"

"The price of fuel, I hear. House prices. That sort of thing."

"You're such a pedant. What's going on in your life at the moment, then?"

"I wanted to ask if you were going to the open day this week." I decide to let the argument about genetics slide on the basis that I've actually missed talking to Alan, even though he's annoying sometimes. Besides, he's fun to have around during college open days, which are a wonderful invention: completely legitimate excuses to miss days of school. The point is not whether one intends to ever attend the third-level institution in question, but whether one would rather be there for the day than sitting in class. What with Alan having done all this before, he's a little bit choosier about the open days he goes to, but the last time we wound up at one together, we ended up in the college bar by two. I am hoping to break that record this time around.

"Yeah," he says slowly, and it's only then that I remember which college his first-preference course was in the last time he filled out the CAO form. And that it is the same college he dropped out of after not getting that first-preference course and not being offered similar courses elsewhere. When did I stop remembering these details about people's lives?

And yet. Well. I know it's got to be hard to not get what you want the first time around, but still, Alan knows exactly what he wants to do. He will do his degree in psychology and then go on to further study until he gets a doctorate of some kind, probably in clinical psychology or neuroscience, though he is allowing for the possibility of finding another area within the field that might sufficiently interest him. It is very difficult to feel sorry for someone who has their entire life planned out.

I wonder how I've managed to surround myself with these smart brilliant people who have these amazing long-term goals. It's really scary. I mean, at least Alan has the excuse of being older and wiser and all that, but Anna's the same age as me. And even Jen, who has no aspirations towards doctorhood, is completely comfortable with her plan to become a primary school teacher. Everyone seems to have something definite to aim for, something to work for.

Maybe that's how you motivate yourself for these exams, by wanting something so badly that you've no choice but to slave away the year. There's got to be *some* reason for all this. If I knew what I wanted then everything would fall into place.

"So do you want to meet up beforehand?" I ask Alan before we start talking about his unrealised dreams or whatever path that conversation might take. I know it still bothers him that he made a mess of things two years ago, but as the year progresses I find myself less sympathetic towards the idea that getting five hundred points is some kind of tragedy. I mean, I understood at the time. I really did. He got his results the summer before I went into fifth year, back in the days when I was in that mindset where anything below 90% was just not good enough. I could practically taste his disappointment. But that was before I really understood how much work it all was. How it doesn't matter if you're supposedly smart, because the Leaving Cert isn't about that at all.

How you can be really smart, like Alan, and still not get the sort of fantastic results that people think you should get, because smart just doesn't count anymore, or maybe it's just that you're not smart enough for this. You've reached your limit. Smartness isn't going to get you anywhere anymore. You're no longer the little kid who always had their hand up in the air before everyone else whenever a question was asked, who knew how to multiply a year before it was taught in school, who could grasp the concept of fractals before starting secondary school. For example.

Alan and I make our plans for Wednesday morning and then I hang up and cross that item off my list. I'll talk to him about the Excuse Party then, see if he wants to come along. I'm not sure if he will, or how much I want him there. Alan and I get on really well – mostly – when it's just us, but I'm not sure how he'd fit in at this thing. Alan is the sort of boy that parents adore (actually, my parents are quite fond of him) and Rob is the sort of boy you'd sneak out of the house for. There's a bit of a difference there. Alan does crazy things occasionally and tells the story for months afterwards; Rob can't even remember all the stuff he gets up to. Alan would like to think of himself as cool; Rob is so cool he doesn't care whether he is or isn't. Alan is reasonably good-looking in a certain light; Rob is utterly delicious. And so on. They are different breeds, and if Alan is in a situation where he doesn't get on with the other guys, then he'll be hanging around with me all night, and that means that I won't have the chance to spend any time alone with Rob, and that is my ultimate goal for Saturday night.

Still, I guess I'd feel bad about not inviting him. He can always bring along a few of his friends. Maybe even James. Anna has yet to declare her undying love for him, and vice-versa, so maybe the vague idea that Alan and I have about the two of them getting together at some point wasn't the best, but perhaps under the right circumstances something could still happen between them. She deserves a little fun in her life.

I run through the list of numbers in my phone one more time, just to see if there's anyone else I should invite. Jen spread the word to Rob and the others, which meant that I didn't have to, which means it's all still very casual and laid-back and not like the pre-Debs where I'd have had to ask him as my official date for the evening. He's just so very much not the type for that kind of formality, it would have been weird. This is much better.

I hover over Emma's number, even though it would probably be really strange asking her via text message instead of in person. I am fairly sure that she's sticking with the pre-Debs route, and that she and Paul will be inseparable all night and nobody else will be able to have any kind of a conversation with them, but we were all friends once upon a time.

It seems I'm just not the sort of person who spends sixth year hanging out with all the same people she was friends with when she was in first year. If I was that sort of person, I'd be like Natalie, deeply believing that it's going to be terribly tragic when we all go our separate ways next year, and determined to make the most of what little time we have left together.

The more and more I think about it the more I realise that I'm not upset about this being my last year of school. I always thought I would be. But I'm not going to miss sitting in class feeling stupid, or watching Laura have all the right answers, or having people talking about grinds and points and mocks and all the rest. I'm not going to miss the teachers, who will only remember their favourites and even then only hazily.

I'm fed up, tired, worn out with the whole thing. Wake me up when June rolls around, I think.

12

Anna

"Is it weird being back?" I ask Alan as we follow the temporary yellow-paper signs to the lecture theatre.

He shrugs. "Not really."

I feel as though I've asked a stupid question.

"But I never had any lectures in here," he continues, "so it's still half-new to me. They don't let finance students anywhere near the science buildings."

"That seems like a reasonable decision," I say, glad that we're able to sort-of have a conversation when it's just the two of us. "Who knows what those business-minded freaks would do, right?"

"Exactly," he says, and launches into detailing a wacky hypothetical scenario. We sit down inside the theatre just as he gets to the part where the actuary and the marketing student have brought their *Frankenstein*-style monster to life. I laugh and occasionally make contributions to the story, but mostly just laugh.

It's turning out to be far less awkward than it could have been. Vicky organised it so that a group of us would meet up at this general talk about making the transition from secondary school to college. I'm not sure how useful that talk was, given that we're still *in* secondary school for the next while and need to do things their way for the time being, but anyway. The one starting here in five minutes is about the health sciences, which I'm hoping will be slightly more informative and relevant. Alan and I were the only two interested; the others are off doing their own thing. I'm glad not to have to wander around on my own but at the same time we've hardly ever been in situations where it's just the two of us, he's more an acquaintance than a friend.

I appreciate the fact that he wraps up the story just as the guy at the podium starts clearing his throat. I would appreciate it even more if everyone else here would stop talking. I mean, come *on*.

When things finally settle down we get a speech on studying at this fine institution and a list of all the wonderful facilities and blah blah blah. Then there's time for questions, where people stick up their hands to ask mostly stupid things like how many points you need for a certain course or what subjects are required or how to go about deferring. What's wrong with these people? The closing date for CAO applications is in less than two months; haven't they read the handbook? And even *glancing* at the college prospectus would answer the rest of their questions.

"Well, what did you think?" Alan asks when it's over and we've fought our way through the crowds out of the theatre.

"I think that was a waste of my time," I say.

"It was fairly pointless," he agrees.

We wander around the stands that have been set up. I pick up a leaflet from the medicine stand and talk to a few med students who seem very casual and laid-back and not at all like people who at some point in the last few years had to study hard enough to get at least five hundred and eighty points.

"It's not as hard as you think as it's going to be," a guy whose nametag identifies him as 'Dan' tells me before I leave, which is meant to be reassuring but isn't. It's completely unnerving talking to these people. They are exactly where I want to be in a couple of years and I can't see anything of myself in them.

When I find Alan and he suggests we move on, it sounds like the greatest idea in the history of the universe. We're outside, debating whether or not to go to a talk about the sports facilities in the college, when someone comes over to say hi; turns out it's a friend of his from school who's now in college here.

I bet it's annoying for the students here to have this day where the place is swarming with secondary school kids. I wish I was on the other side of the dividing line.

When the guy leaves, I realise that I have no interest in the sports talk, or any other talk designed for us. I don't want to be a part of the crowd who are getting in the way of the college students or asking stupid questions or being condescended to and told it's all going to be fine. I think about leaving now, and going to do my Christmas shopping; it seemed like a good idea to try to get it out of the way today.

"I have a thought," Alan says.

"What's this thought?" I ask.

"James is finished today at twelve."

I check my watch. It's a quarter to. "And?" I say.

"And he thinks we should go for drinks."

"At twelve *noon?* On a *Wednesday?"*

"Which sounded a little too decadent even for me," Alan says, "but I think Vicky wants to go for drinks at some stage anyway, and . . . ah, what do you say?"

What I should say is that it's a ridiculous idea, and that if I'm not going to get anything else from this open day then I should go and get my Christmas shopping sorted out or do something else productive. I mean, it's still technically *morning.*

Me saying yes would be giving into peer pressure, and I am far too old for that sort of thing. I am not going to consume alcohol in the middle of the day in the middle of the week just because the opportunity has presented itself. It would be irresponsible and immature.

On the other hand, James knows I'm around today, because he asked me yesterday evening if I was coming in to the open day and said that he might see me around. And going for drinks would be an excellent way of seeing him, wouldn't it?

"Let's go," I say to Alan, and by five to twelve we are both sitting down with a sandwich and a pint in front of us.

Vicky arrives two minutes after we send her a text. "I'm impressed," she laughs as she sits down next to Alan, leaving the seat next to me available for that very nice young man who should be here any minute. I'm trying not to fidget or hyperventilate or do anything too obviously panicky. I remind myself to drink slowly.

"I think this is good," Vicky says as she looks through her bag. "I mean, if we end up coming here, this is probably where we'll spend most of our time, right?"

"Well, *you* will, probably," Alan says, which stops me from getting annoyed at her for saying something so stupid and buying into that cliché about college life. I mean, the bar is mostly empty. Clearly *some* people are busy studying or going to classes or having non-alcoholic lunches.

Vicky grins and, after finding her wallet, goes up to get a drink. Out of the corner of my eye I think I maybe see someone who might be James but I don't want to turn around and make eye contact. My heart is pounding.

I clench my fists underneath the table. This is ridiculous. I see him every week. How can he possibly still have this effect on me? How can I possibly keep getting this nervous? At this rate of going I'm not going to make it to June in one piece.

Vicky returns with her drink. "Okay, so Jen and Luke are going to join us later, and Sinéad's gone off for lunch with the latest love of her life, so I don't know if we'll be seeing her at all. How did you guys get on?"

I shrug. "It was all right."

"I'd say mind-numbingly dull, actually," Alan says.

"Yes, those were the words I was looking for." Is he here yet? Can I look at my watch without Vicky and Alan noticing and guessing why I'm doing it?

"Well, I had a conversation about the meaning of life with a philosophy student, so I'm happy," Vicky says.

"Did you discover what the meaning of life is?" Alan wants to know.

"I didn't, but I do now know that I never want to study philosophy. Ever."

"What's this?"

James.

In the split second my attention was diverted towards Alan and Vicky, he somehow managed to appear next to us. Maybe it's his hair. Maybe it really is magical.

"I've been discussing the meaning of life," Vicky tells him as he sits down next to me. "And now I'm here."

"Needed a drink after all that, huh?" he says.

"Exactly," she laughs.

Here's the thing: I know very well that Vicky is utterly besotted with Rob and therefore not interested in James in the slightest. But to the casual observer it might seem very much like they're flirting with one another.

I'm not jealous, really. I just wish I found it that easy to talk to him.

13

Vicky

"Yeah, a lot of people find it really tough," James says, taking a pause to eat the chips he's speared with his fork. "If you make it through first year you'll be fine, though."

He's talking about his course. I know from the way he says it, and from knowing him, that he's one of the people who does not find it tough. I'm not in the mood for this today.

"That's the same with a lot of courses, though, isn't it?" I say. "Anna, what's the one where two-thirds of people drop out before the end of first year?"

She shrugs. "Oh, I don't know. Computer science or something. There's a lot of science courses with really high drop-out rates."

"Someone's been doing their research," James notes, looking amused. Anna blushes and promptly changes the subject.

I'm glad to be talking about something else. I wonder if Anna's as intimidated by being here as I am. I can't remember the last time I heard her say I-don't-know to any kind of college-related query. I think maybe being actually being here in person instead of just reading about it and having all the facts is what's making her shy. Theory and reality are two very different things.

I should have gone with her and Alan to their talk, or followed Sinéad to the one about studying arts subjects, or done something other than wander around and realise just how much is out there. Open days are much more fun when you're not taking them seriously, or when you've a vague idea what you want to do.

Everything looks so interesting and yet so difficult. I could study political science or a language, which sounds fascinating until I remember that I have no particular aptitude for these things. But then again I don't seem to have the aptitude for any of the courses I've been looking at up until now. I am not James, obviously brilliant in one particular area, and I don't want to be one of those people dropping out of college before the end of first year. College is where everyone is a little fish in a big pond and I already feel tiny.

"Ah, James, it's not even the end of term yet," a girl with pink streaks in her hair says as she approaches, shaking her head. "Starting the celebrations early?"

"Something like that," he says. "Feel like joining us? These guys are here for the open day."

"I'm doing the camera work for this group project later, so I think it *might* be best if I was sober for that," she grins. "Anyway, I'm meeting Róisín for lunch, so I won't keep her waiting. Good to meet you guys," she nods towards us. "See you later, James."

"She's cute," Alan says when she's gone.

"She's taken. She's very taken," James sighs.

"What's she studying?" Anna asks.

"Media studies," James says. "Such a waffly course. But she's cool."

"You're such a snob," I say to James, half laughing and half genuinely annoyed. He just shrugs. I wonder how well he would get on in such a course. I read the leaflet earlier. It sounds like the sort of thing I'd be terrible at. I wonder if James is just one of those people who are good at everything they put their mind to, like Laura. Like Anna.

It's better not to think about those people. What I need to do is just accept that I'm not cut out to be brilliant at exams, at school, at this learning thing. That's just not who I am.

I am Vicky, I am seventeen, I am sitting in a college

bar at lunch time with a drink in my hand and I am sitting with two people I care about very much plus one I would probably like more if he wasn't so good at something I really wish I could be good at again. But apart from that, it's not a bad way to spend a Wednesday.

We order another round of drinks and Jen and Luke join us, and then a few of James's friends arrive, and I start thinking about Rob and wishing he was here. Rob thinks today is a waste of time. I can sort of see his point, but I wish he was here anyway. He'd like this, I think, sitting around here, laughing and talking, telling ridiculous anecdotes and wandering off on tangents.

This is what I want to have now, this freedom, not all this petty pathetic school stuff. I feel like I could stay here forever, like it's one of those parties where it's late at night but no one wants to leave because there are so many in-jokes going on and so much being talked about that you'd regret missing out on this. It surprises me when we walk out into daylight, even though it's fading quickly.

We get the bus home. I'm sleepy by the time we arrive at my stop, and it's getting darker, which makes the slight tipsiness feel more acceptable. The parents aren't home yet, but Tara is, stretched out on the couch watching TV with an empty popcorn bag lying on the floor and a half-empty mug balancing precariously next to her elbow.

I sit down in an armchair and she glares at me.

"What?" I say.

"I'm *watching* this."

"I'm not doing anything."

She makes an unintelligible noise and storms out. I can hear her stomping up the stairs to her bedroom. I would feel far more sympathetic towards her if she didn't have a TV in her own room. And if she wasn't so crazy. There's no way I was that insane when I was her age.

I take over the abandoned couch and flip through the channels. I feel as though I could fall asleep right here. I think about all the homework I have to do, about how I should really start studying soon, and even the thought of it saps the rest of my energy. Tomorrow. I'll do it tomorrow. Or next week. Or after Christmas. But soon. Probably. Maybe.

I'm tired. I'm just so *tired.*

14

Anna

Oh, that was a stupid idea. When I get home I take some aspirin and take a bottle of water up to my room. It's not that I'm drunk, just not clear-headed enough to do any work. I had two pints and then switched over to water, leaving me just sober enough to appreciate the fact that everyone else on the bus home knew very well that we were a bunch of inebriated teenagers.

I hate the thought that some stranger could look at me and my friends and get the idea that we're the sort of people who aren't going to do anything with their lives. I mean, drunk in the middle of the day. That says something. And we're letting it say something. I should have stuck to the plan.

Except, all right, James was there and seeing him was a good thing, obviously, but he's clearly into that girl with pink hair, pining after her, so –

I'm such an idiot. I mean, of course he's interested in someone. Not that I was hoping – I wasn't hoping for anything. I know nothing's ever going to happen. I know it.

I should have done my Christmas shopping. I should be in college and have dyed hair and be cool and casual and confident, clearly. I wonder if I'll ever be like that, if you ever feel as cool as you seem to others.

Moping around is not a valid reason for not working, I remind myself. I turn on the computer and check my email, then begin a reply to the one Lily sent me a few days ago. Penny and Noel are going away the weekend after next and Lily wonders if I want to stay over that weekend. Denise keeps staying out till all hours of the night with her boyfriend and Lily hates being alone in the house.

Normally I try to be prompt about responding to emails but I've been pondering over this one. On the one hand, there is a part of me that still thinks she's ten and will ask how high when Lily says jump. On the other hand, I could be spending that weekend studying.

I know that no one can reasonably be expected to

spend every waking hour studying. It's not physically or mentally possible. You have to take breaks, take time off, relax, unwind, whatever. But where do you draw the line between taking breaks and just putting off all the work you're supposed to be doing? Today's a break. Saturday night – and possibly Sunday morning, if I'm drinking – will be a break.

I knock on the door of the spare room, where my dad is reading a book by some guy named Derrida. I've learned the hard way that it's easier if I avoid asking him what anything is about. He's so enthusiastic, even when he's criticising something for being too abstract or wacky or whatever it might be. I suppose you have to be when you're deciding to go and study part-time instead of just falling into college after school.

I am torn between being jealous of my parents and being glad I'm not them. It's tough going back into education after having got out of the habit of studying, and I know that even though college isn't like school I'd find it horrible to be in a class with people so much younger than me. Dad's course, because it's part-time, has a lot of older people in it, but Mom did hers full-time. I can't imagine being in my forties and having classes with teenagers, doing the same work that they're doing, sitting the same exams.

At the same time, mature students do not have to

fulfil the same requirements that school-leavers do. And colleges take other things into account. It's not just based on this one exam. You are not just an anonymous number who either gets the points or doesn't, end of story.

"Lily wants me to stay over with her next weekend," I say.

"Next weekend, next weekend . . . is that the weekend Penny and Noel are in Cork?"

"Yeah. What d'you think?"

"What do *I* think?"

"I'm debating whether or not to go."

"Well, what do you want to do?" he asks.

I want him to tell me that it's okay to take a break and that I shouldn't feel guilty about it. I am such a child, wanting my dad to make these decisions for me.

"I don't know," I say. "I have to see what else I have going on."

He nods. "How was the open day?"

I shrug. "It was all right. I was talking to a couple of the med students."

"That's good. Were they helpful?"

"Sort of. I think they've forgotten what it's like to be still in school. I mean, I think it's the kind of thing where once you're into the course, that's the worst of it over, you know?"

"Ah, I don't know about that. I remember Seán always found it very tough, when he was getting his degree."

Seán is my dad's cousin and the sort of person we see at funerals and christenings only. He is ten years older than Dad, which means he's sixty, which means he started college over forty years ago, back in the days when a handful of honours got you in.

Sometimes I cannot believe that my father can wrap his head around philosophy but can't grasp the fact that the educational system has changed since he was my age. Of course medicine is going to be tough. You're responsible for people's *lives*, it has to be.

But you're there because you want to be, because you know that being a doctor is absolutely what you want to do with your life, and worth studying for, and that the course is what you've chosen to do. You're not there because someone's decided that the best way to ensure someone's suitability for third-level education is to test them on a number of subjects which may or may not be relevant to what they want to study. It will be hard but it'll be easier than *this*.

It will be, right?

I change the subject and ask Dad if he wants to watch another episode of *ER* tonight. I might as well, it's not like I'm going to get any work done. We consult with Mom on the matter, who suggests adding an order from the take-away into the mix.

I wonder what James would think if he could see me now, sitting at home with my parents, sharing chips and chicken pieces and commenting on the complete implausibility of that patient's symptoms to cries of "It's called dramatic license, Anna!" I bet the girl with the pink streaks spends her nights doing more exciting things.

After the DVD goes back in its case, I finish the email to Lily and let her know I'll be there that weekend. I think really what I'm hoping for is a lesson in how to be grown-up. It's stupid, I know, but it helps me make my mind up and that's another thing crossed off the To Do list.

15

Vicky

"Maybe I should dye my hair," Anna muses.

"You've gorgeous hair, don't touch it," Jen says.

We're at Jen's house, a place I seem to be spending more time in than my own home, and Jen is looking wistfully at Anna's hair. "You don't *need* to do anything with your hair. I sort of hate you."

"Thanks," Anna laughs. Her hair, dark and naturally straight, is out of its usual ponytail for tonight. Jen and I have spent the past forty-five minutes doing our hair. She's curled hers and I've been using her GHD, and even though I've never wanted to become one of those compulsive hair-straighteners there's something wonderfully satisfying about having your hair looking like you want it to look for once. Anna ran a brush through her hair and she was finished.

I don't know what it is, exactly, but there's something envy-inducing about people who can get things effortlessly. It's like anyone can be beautiful if they put in enough work, anyone can reach that destination if they try really hard, so to be able to get there without all that work makes you superior. Natural gifts trump hard work. You're only beautiful if you're naturally beautiful. You're only smart if you're naturally smart. It means less if you have to work for it.

The Tiger Bar is just down the road from Jen's house. The Excuse Party starts at half-eight, officially; we're supposed to be there at eight just to make sure everything's ok.

It's half-seven and we are in make-up application mode, except for Anna who's been ready for ages and has time, apparently, for ponderings on whether she should dye her hair or not.

"Is Luke meeting us there?" I ask as I put on eyeliner. It's a delicate operation. Jen offered to do it for me but I can't stand anyone else putting anything near my eyes. It's bad enough when I have to do it to myself.

"Yeah, he said he'll try to get there for eight," Jen says. "Which means I might see him by nine, if I'm lucky. Do you think I should get him a watch for Christmas? Would that be too pointed?"

"Just pointed enough," Anna says.

I poke myself in the eye twice before I'm finished. There's a reason I'm not the sort of person who wears make-up every day. I don't have the patience to do this every single morning. But it's worth making the effort for tonight. I have a new dress and new shoes and there's no point in wearing those and then not putting on a bit of make-up and doing my hair.

Even if I'm not naturally beautiful, when I look in the mirror I feel like I might be pretty tonight. I could be pretty, fun Vicky. Not debater Vicky, not good-at-maths Vicky, but party Vicky. Desirable Vicky. The male of the species, unlike the university entrance system, doesn't care how many A's you get in your exams. This is the real world, and in the real world good hair matters more than good marks.

At least as far as Rob is concerned. But I can't see anyone using their IQ in a chat-up line and being successful. Unless maybe they were at a Mensa meeting.

I wonder briefly if Laura is a member of Mensa before moving onto more pleasant thoughts, like Rob and the fact that I look, well, if not beautiful, then reasonably attractive in my dress.

We arrive in the bar at five past eight. We have downstairs booked. It's depressingly empty at the moment, and I panic for a moment – what if we don't have the numbers to make this into a good night?

What if it's a pitiful attempt at trying to be different?

Then I think of the list, and it's all okay again. If even half the people who said they'd come turn up, we'll have a good crowd. We order our drinks and wait.

Alan arrives at half-eight on the dot, with two of the guys who are repeating their exams in the same place he is. Anna doesn't seem impressed. I can't say I'm overly thrilled to be around three repeat students either. It's sort of depressing. They're only here for the one drink anyway, before heading into town.

As they're leaving, Rob arrives with his friends. I pretend that I haven't noticed and hug Alan in a way that could be interpreted as more than a just-friends gesture by onlookers.

"You're pathetic," Alan says into my ear, but not in a completely mean way.

"Have a good night," I say sweetly.

He rolls his eyes and follows his friends up the stairs.

"Vicky, my dear, you look lovely," Rob says. I know enough to know he's joking about the 'my dear'. Unfortunately. "Not like this tramp over here," he adds, poking Jen, who elbows him right back.

"You look reasonably okay yourself," I laugh.

He's not overly dressed up – the group that have just arrived, two girls from our year accompanied by boys I don't know, look as though they're ready for the actual Debs – but even the shirt is a change from the casual about-to-disintegrate-in-the-wash stuff I'm used to seeing him in. And he's wearing actual proper grown-up shoes. I suspect they might be his school shoes – they're a little too scuffed to be fancy-occasion-only footwear – but it's still surprising. Different.

It feels like tonight might actually turn out to be one of those nights that you look back on fondly, one of those sixth-year best-days-of-your-life experiences that we're supposed to be having.

The more people arrive, the more it feels like this. There's no one really unpleasant here, no one who might have muttered something vicious to you at some point in the last few years. There are, of course, plenty of people who have probably muttered something vicious *about* you, but everyone bitches about everyone else in school at least once. Six years with the same people will do that. The minor annoyances, like the in-house politics of the debating crowd, are fading away.

Maybe it's the warm-fuzzy feeling of a memorable event in progress, or maybe it's the alcopops I'm working my way through. Maybe all memorable events are really just standard hilarious drunken nights in more expensive outfits.

Rob, Jen, Luke and Chris are competing to see who

can tell the dirtiest joke when Anna says, "Hey, Laura's here."

I look at the bottle in front of me – WKD Blue – and wonder if somehow I've already lost track of how many I've had. Laura's here? That has to be some kind of hallucination brought on by overly sugary vodka-based beverages, right?

Jen and Anna go over and say hi to Laura, who a) looks fantastic and b) is accompanied by a rather delicious guy who c) appears to be totally infatuated with her. He is gazing adoringly at her. Which I suppose is understandable, because Laura out of her school uniform and out of her teacher's pet guise does look like the sort of girl boys should adore. I wonder if her hair – blonde, wavy, very fairytale princess-ish – looks like that without any effort, if she could wear it like that into school every day if she wanted to but keeps it tied up for the sake of practicality. It is sort of sickening how pretty she looks.

"What did she do to you?" Rob asks, grinning at me.

"Oh, nothing," I say.

"What, are you ignoring her?" Chris says, just tuning in.

"No," I say, "I'm just staying here with you charming gentlemen instead."

"We're honoured," Luke says.

"She did something," Rob insists in my ear, persistent and flirty. "Don't tell me she stole that lad from you, did she?"

She stole nothing from me, apart from my status as Ms Black's favourite maths student. It's so ridiculous. I shouldn't care about it. It's just not fair that she's here, even though yes Jen invited her and yes Jen and Anna get along with her and yes she's mostly a nice person apart from being painfully brilliant.

I giggle. "She didn't steal him. I've never seen him before in my life, and he's not my type, anyway."

Rob, voice low, picks up on his cue. "So what is your type, then?"

We are now close enough to make the answer to that question fairly obvious. I kiss him. It's that simple.

By the time Jen and Anna return to our little cluster, Rob and I have already moved into the realm of the coupled, sitting half in each other's laps and exchanging saliva every few minutes.

I am party Vicky. I am desirable Vicky. We dance for a few songs, until there's a group trip out into the freezing cold to alleviate the smokers' nicotine habits. I venture out with them but *fuck* it's cold. This dress is not designed for December and my coat's inside under a tangle of other coats and I am nowhere near drunk enough to either ignore the impending frostbite or to think that it would be a reasonable price to pay for an extra fifteen minutes at Rob's side.

Back inside, in the blissful warmth, Laura and her date / boyfriend / whatever are coming up the stairs.

"Hey," she says to me. "You look great, I love that dress."

I smile right back. "Thanks! You look fantastic. Having a good night so far?"

"Yeah, absolutely. This was such a good idea."

I walk down the stairs thinking that maybe we could actually be friends, which is a sure sign that alcohol and kisses have combined to stop my brain cells from working properly. It's so much easier not to be jealous of her when we're not in school and when I too have a boy who looks adoringly at me. Every day should be like this. People dressed up, and music you can dance to, and a certain kind of energy in the air that tells you that this is a memory in the making.

This is the stuff that really matters. People, not exams. People.

I say hi to Jessica, to Sinéad and her boyfriend, who've just arrived, to a few of the others I haven't talked to yet. Rob alerts me to his return with a kiss on my neck, and we dance again. More drinking. More kissing. And hands going all over the place. We are not the only groping pair in the vicinity, not by a long shot, but I know there are at least a couple of raised eyebrows. People who only know me from school do not necessarily think of me as the kind of girl who is in favour of public displays of affection, I suspect. Some of them may even still think of me as smart Vicky, well-behaved organiser girl.

There is a thrill in the idea of being shocking, mixed in with the delight of actually being with Rob, not just flirting and hoping and dreaming.

Another smoking break. The crowd is starting to thin out. It's late and my feet hurt. When I go to get another drink, Sinéad asks if I'll get her a water while I'm there. Is it the water-drinking stage of the night already? I've missed people leaving. Anna's vanished. Jessica's gone. I'll text them later. No, tomorrow, in case they're already asleep or something.

The bar staff gently nudge us upstairs with the rest of their customers, presumably so they can get started cleaning up our mess. It serves as a cue for half of the remaining Excuse Party crowd to start saying their goodbyes, so we all end up leaving. I'm not ready to go, not ready for the night to be over just yet, but as usual Jen is willing to step up and be the enabling hostess in our lives.

This, I suppose, is how Rob and I end up in the spare room in Jen's house. The others are still drinking downstairs – Jen, Luke, and a few of the guys are sharing a bottle or two of wine and being mostly-quiet for the sake of Jen's sleeping parents – but we are here.

We're all crashing at Jen's tonight. And it's late, close enough to morning to just fall asleep and not be any kind of loser for giving into the tiredness. But the thing about the tiredness is that it melts away as soon as I've slipped off my shoes and slid underneath the covers next to that utterly delicious boy who's been all over me all night.

Really, when you think about it, there's only one move that makes sense in this scenario.

"Ready to go to sleep?" he asks me, and even in the dark I can tell he's grinning.

"Absolutely," I say, and we laugh our way into a kiss.

16

Anna

What I decide on Sunday morning is that I should just stop drinking. Entirely. At least until the exams are over. Possibly for life.

Here's the really obvious and yet frequently ignored thing about alcohol: it leaves you unable to function properly the following day. Maybe it's only feeling vaguely ill when you first get up, or the hint of a headache that haunts you all day, or maybe it's a full-blown unable-to-get-out-of-bed situation, the kind of hangover I've never experienced personally but have heard tales of, but unless you're one of those lucky people who escapes the effects entirely, you can't do the sort of things that you can when you've had a good night's sleep. You can't, for example, force your brain to take in information the way it can when it's working properly. You can't concentrate on anything for longer than a few minutes. You can't be productive.

I don't want to wake up in June and realise that all my weekends have been lost to post-nights-out unproductiveness.

Alcohol is also a depressant. Which we all know and somehow forget about because of its initial happiness-inducing properties. Which means that sometimes, if it's a night out, and if absolutely everyone is paired up and paired off and has their mouth glued to someone else's or their hand in another's, and you're alone, and you are having exactly the kind of miserable experience you were worried about having, you may slip out of a gathering early and walk home with tears streaming down your face.

And even though you know the next morning that all that sobbing and feeling pathetic and lonely was due to the mind-altering effects of alcohol, you still feel like crap.

So. I'm not drinking again.

Besides, it's probably not the best idea for future doctors (oh I hope I hope I hope) to risk liver damage and all those other alcohol-related things we'll end up treating people for.

I consult my notebook because it feels like something exam-related to do that can be accomplished even with the dull throbbing in my head. My last biology test, 94. Stupid mistake. Chemistry, 100, but that was a very straightforward one, nothing tricky about it. Accounting, 100. Maths, 83, the best in the class but not good enough. A B1, eighty-five points in the real thing. Not good enough.

I got an A2 in my last French listening test. It is that sort of thing which keeps me from dropping down to pass. The possibility of needing to count it, in case of an unexpected disaster.

I consider moving down to pass maths, except that it would feel like a failure, not taking the higher-level course. It would be like taking the easy way out. I've managed for the past year and a bit doing the higher-level course. I can hang on in there. I don't want to do anything I will regret in a year's time.

I will not drop down to pass. In anything. I am getting by in French and it is one of those subjects where there isn't a huge variance in the two levels anyway so it would be completely silly of me to switch classes. I will not let myself be one of those people who make stupid decisions when under pressure. And I will not let myself spend the rest of the year recovering from nights out that are far more trouble than they're worth.

I have goals. Now I just need to achieve them. That's how it works.

17

Vicky

Jen's dad is apparently a saint in human form and makes breakfast for all of us the next morning. I am not a fan of fry-ups at the best of times, having been a vegetarian since I was fourteen, but while I can usually understand people's meat cravings, this particular one disgusts me. There is still an awful lot of alcohol churning around in my stomach and my brain and I barely trust myself to get through the slice of dry toast in front of me.

Meanwhile, Rob, the love of my life, or at least the lusted-after of last night, is devouring rashers as though there's no tomorrow. I look away to avoid running the risk of throwing up all over him, which would definitely ruin whatever it is we have going on now. Whatever kind of 'us' we are.

There's a very large part of me that just wants to

go home and collapse into bed. I didn't get much sleep last night. No, correct that: *we* didn't get very much sleep last night, and phrasing it that way makes me smile. I bite down on my lower lip to minimise looking like a grinning idiot, even though everyone at this table – Jen's dad excluded – is well aware that myself and Rob had the spare room to ourselves last night. Why wouldn't something have happened, right? Dancing, drunk, desirable Vicky is not uptight about such things in the way that some girls are. She seizes the day rather than clinging to stupid ideas about waiting for a certain amount of time to have lapsed before it's acceptable, according to some ridiculous standard, to sleep with someone.

Rob still being here is the reason that I have not gone home. Rob is here and I don't want to miss out on anything.

After breakfast Jen suggests television, and we all settle down to watch this stand-up comedy thing she has on DVD, apart from Chris, who goes home. I watch him leave, slightly envious, but then Rob sits next to me on the couch and we snuggle up together. I'm still in my dress from last night, with a borrowed hoodie from Jen keeping me warm, but Rob's arms around me don't hurt, either. Being touched, little bits of intimacy like this – it makes me content in a way that even tiredness and hangovers can't ruin.

We end up staying until it's dark outside, not that the onset of darkness is hugely significant this late in the year. Rob and I are going in completely different directions so we part ways at the end of Jen's road, with an appropriate public display of affection, and then the group disperses. Luke and I share a stretch of a road within an estate before I'm on my own entirely, and then it's another few minutes before I get home.

"You've missed dinner," is the first thing my dad says to me when I walk in the door.

"Oh. I've had food," I say. If tortilla chips, which we had with a dip none of us could quite identify while watching a programme about bridesmaids who've run off with grooms just before the vows, count as food.

He frowns. "We didn't think you'd be out all day," he says.

My mum chooses this moment to join us out in the hallway. "Vicky! You finally decided to come home."

It's not that they're giving out to me. It's not like that. It's just that they're being pointed.

Last night, on the way back to Jen's house, I sent a text message to both their phones to let them know where I'd be. I even got Jen to read over it before I sent it to make sure it didn't contain any obvious drunken spelling mistakes. I fully embraced their "Let us know where you are, no matter what time it is" policy and even that, apparently, is not enough. I should have been home for dinner. Probably breakfast. Not because I've really missed anything but because home is where their children are supposed to be.

I exhale loudly, knowing very well I sound more like Tara than me at that moment.

"I'm going to make some coffee," I say, heading for the kitchen. "Anyone want some?"

The parents follow. My mum will have a cup. My dad contemplates the matter for a few minutes before deciding that it's too late in the day for it. I wonder if that's another pointed remark.

"Going to get some study done this evening?" my dad asks as the water begins to boil.

"Nope," I say, hoping that will put an end to it. Sunday evening. Studying. Jesus.

"Are you getting much done?" my mum wants to know. "In general. How's it going?"

"Have you asked Tara how it's going?" I reply.

"Tara's not the point, Vicky," my dad says, not for the first time. This is usually the stage when my parents begin talking to me as though I'm three years old.

"We just want to know," my mum says, "how you're getting on . . ."

". . . we're your parents, it's our business to know . . ."

". . . we just want to make sure that you're putting in the work . . ."

". . . you've been going out a lot, and we're just concerned . . ."

What am I supposed to tell them? Telling them that I haven't been studying, that I doubt my very capacity for study, would not be a wise move. Reassuring them that everything is under control and that I've plenty of work done would be equally foolish, leaving them with expectations for me. Either way they'll be disappointed. It's just a matter of when.

"It's fine," I interrupt them. "Go focus on your other daughter, for God's sake."

They helpfully remind me that Tara is not sitting her Leaving Cert this year. They also wish to know if I have decided what I'm putting down on my CAO form.

"I don't know yet," I say honestly.

"Have you talked to your guidance counsellor?" my mum asks.

"You should definitely go in for a chat," my dad advises.

No one goes in 'for a chat' to Mrs Fitzpatrick. She calls you in once a year to have an awkward discussion about how you're getting on, as though anyone would willingly discuss such things with someone who can't remember who you are unless they have their folder on you in front of them. She also believes in getting students to research the various options available to them rather than providing them with helpful information, and is mostly likely to say something along the lines of "I think College X used to offer Course Y, but I'm not sure they do anymore . . . you should go look that up."

She's two years from retirement, apparently. I suppose that explains why she has no interest in keeping up with any of it, but there's no way I would go and chat to her about what I want to put down on the CAO. What I want to do with my life.

"She's not very good," I try to explain to the parents.

They talk about how they're sure she's not that bad, which is exactly the problem with my parents. They are sure about things they have no right to be sure of. Things that they are completely clueless about.

Me saying that Mrs Fitzpatrick doesn't really know what she's doing is not some immature reaction to someone in authority I don't like. I am an almost-adult who knows very well that she is incompetent at her job, who knows that she gives out inaccurate information (admittedly only because Anna has often pointed this out), who is frustrated that there isn't someone in school who might say reassuring things to me about the future.

Me thinking that my parents are out of touch is not me being a typical teenager. It is me recognising a reality.

Their insistence on seeing me like a typical teenager at moments like these is why I end up storming up to my room. I hate that I've just acted out that cliché. I hate that they'll be smugly thinking that they have me all figured out now, that they're right.

There's more to life than exams, parents. More to life than studying and points and CAO forms. Much more. And you don't know me nearly as well as you think you do.

18

Anna

I wake up to sickening cramps at five a.m. on Monday morning, which at least explains the over-emotional thing on Saturday night.

School seems exceptionally unappealing right now. I let myself contemplate the possibility of staying at home, wrapped up warm and sufficiently numbed with painkillers, for a second. Only a second. Then the Big Picture voice in my head kicks in.

This is the Big Picture: you can't scrawl "I had cramps that day" as an excuse on your script. It will not get you any marks. You could spend the entire year writhing in agony and unless you fall into a certain category that gets you extra marks or extra time or whatever, it doesn't matter. Not on the day.

Right now I hate the Big Picture. But I get out of bed anyway.

Being up early means I can get most of this evening's work done before I go to school. I put all the stuff we did last week in Irish into note format. The influence of other languages – Latin, English, French – on the Irish language, complete with example words. I will never need to know this in real life. And the '*Stair na Gaeilge*' question on Paper 2 is worth very little, for the amount you're supposed to know.

I read a chapter of my chemistry revision book while I eat breakfast. I tend to think that revision books are mostly the lazy student's way of feeling like they're more prepared than they really are, but the chemistry syllabus lends itself to being easily condensed in this style. Definitions, laws, properties, reactions, equations, experiments. It's gloriously straightforward.

By the time I get to school I feel accomplished. Not even nine o'clock and already I have things ticked off my list for today. That sense of elation dies about two minutes into the morning maths class, when Miss Gormley seems to forget how numbers work. She calculates five cubed to equal fifteen and then wonders why the solution she's written up on the board doesn't quite match up with the answer in the book.

I make a mental note to relate this story to James

tomorrow night. Every few weeks I try to mention some incident which illustrates just how hopeless Miss Gormley is, so that he understands that I'm not just some bumbling idiot.

Miss Gormley. I am irritated by teachers who use Miss or Mrs. Even in a title they still find a way to make it about their love lives. Unmarried or married. Single or taken.

I will be Ms Foster. Then Dr Foster. There's a nursery rhyme about a Dr Foster, the guy who steps in a puddle. When you're a kid you know, right from the start, that 'Dr' must be a man. Because it always is, in those things.

I will be Dr Foster, and no one will be able to tell from that title if I am married or not, or if I am female or not. I will not be Miss Foster, ever, and I will not stand in front of a class of sixth years and make stupid mistakes without realising it, and I will not find myself settling for a job that I'm not cut out for or don't want, which is so obviously what Miss Gormley has done.

I hate being in this class not just because it does not facilitate any kind of learning in the slightest, but because it means watching someone who is exactly the kind of someone I do not want to be in twenty years' time. I want to be competent. I want to be – well, brilliant.

Brilliant. The word sneaks up on me but slides smoothly into place in my brain. Such a non-specific, non-concrete goal, but a true one nonetheless.

I wonder if that means I really am *very ambitious*, then.

It certainly feels ambitious, in the sense of dreaming beyond your capabilities, to want to be brilliant when you've been placed in this particular maths class. I doodle in the margin of my page, lines and triangles and quadrilaterals that are nowhere near the formalities of the *xy*-plane.

How I am ever going to get an A1 in this subject?

Next class is French. Unlike the maths classes, which are divided into pass and honours based on Junior Cert results but then divided further by the alphabet rather than grades, French is entirely streamed. A B in the Junior Cert gets you into the second class, so that I sit with Jen and three seats in front of Emma, instead of with the acknowledged brainboxes like Vicky and Laura and the rest in the top class.

Having a decent teacher in the form of 'Mademoiselle' (she insists we call her this while in class, even though she is Ms Reynolds to her history students and to the school at large) makes this slightly more bearable.

The theme of the chat Jen and I have while everyone else is arriving mostly focuses on the

Excuse Party and its aftermath and how *cute* Vicky and Rob were yesterday. Apparently a bunch of them went back to Jen's place after the festivities died down.

"You should've come," Jen says.

Yeah. Maybe I should have. Maybe I should have stayed around and been included. Except that I didn't feel included even when I was there. But maybe things would have changed. Maybe it would have all worked out well and I'd have been part of the story instead of hearing about it later.

Maybe I'd have even kissed one of the boys or – something. Some kind of drunken silliness to let me have some kind of love-life-related story to tell, even if the someone I really want to kiss prefers cool college girls.

Deep down I know I don't really want that. I don't want any of those boys and I don't want something meaningless and I don't really regret not having stayed up all night partying.

This little part of me feeling like I really genuinely *should* have been there is entirely hormonal and therefore should not be taken seriously.

I remind myself of that throughout the week, as the Excuse Party is analysed and debated and discussed over break and lunch. Who turned up and who got together and who broke up. Natalie and the rest of the pre-Debs crowd are not in the least bit happy at how their own event turned out. Plenty of people from the year still turned up to their thing, but not everyone did. It wasn't quite the whole-year-bonding experience that they were hoping for.

I personally don't know what else they expected. I hear mutterings in the corridors in between classes, people complaining about how there are *divisions* in the year now, as though before all of this we really were one big happy family. It's so stupid. We are here to learn, not to *bond*.

I am one of those quiet people who are mostly invisible and therefore assumed to be in favour of whatever the majority has decided, until things like the confrontation with Natalie happen. I don't stand out.

I swallow any angst that this line of thought might produce. This is the Big Picture: you only need to stand out in one way for college purposes, and that is academically.

I think about Alan, Mr Involved, and remind myself that I am doing the right thing here.

But I still turn up at Lily's house at the weekend with the faint hope that this counts as doing something, being someone interesting or exciting, being *someone*.

19

Vicky

My life after the Excuse Party weekend: quietly smiling to myself a lot. Drifting and daydreaming my way through school. Not coming in for that horrible double class of geography on Tuesday morning and marvelling at how easy and ordinary it is to turn up to school late, instead of some kind of crisis situation. Chatting to people in between classes, being pleasant, being easily pleased.

After school: more daydreaming, exchanging of text messages, time spent online leaving flirtatious comments for one another so as to make it obvious to everyone that there's an 'us'. Jen and Sinéad put a bunch of photos up from the Excuse Party and I select one of them – me, in my dress, laughing, with Rob's arms around my waist and a drink in my hand – as my profile picture. I look pretty, and happy, and it makes me smile every time I log in and see that Vicky grinning back at me.

On Friday night there's a group of us back in the Tiger Bar, and even though I spend most of the night in the toilets with a tearful Jen, who is considering – not for the first time, but more seriously than ever before – ending things with Luke, it still counts as a good night out, somehow. With friends, with Rob, with these people I have come to care about. This is what it's supposed to be like.

I float home and fall into bed with my left shoe still on.

20

Anna

When I arrive Lily is in the middle of a crisis. I know this because the first words she says to me are: "Anna, I'm in the middle of a crisis. Help. Please. Just – help."

"Can I take my coat off first?" I ask, stupidly. It's the only thing I can think of.

With my coat added to the collection on the rack, my bag left under the stairs, and the kettle on (tea is good for crises, I made countless cups of tea for my parents after my grandfather died), I hover in the kitchen and wait for Lily to fill me in on the nature of the aforementioned crisis.

"My sister," she says slowly, "is an *idiot*."

"Is she around? What's she done this time?" I ask.

Denise is sitting the Junior Cert this year. I imagine school-centred scandal. Cheating. Failing something. Skipping classes to go smoke behind the bike sheds, if her school has such places, with her boyfriend.

Lily puts her hands on her hips, a gesture which makes me suddenly eight years old again, being told that we're going to play hairdressers instead of cops and robbers because she's the oldest. "She might be pregnant."

There's a dramatic pause and I know I should say something, only I can't think of anything that's not stupid. She's little Denise. She's – well, she has a boyfriend, but she wouldn't sleep with him, would she?

She's fifteen. Don't be an idiot, I snap at myself, fifteen-year-olds have sex. Just because I didn't. Just because no one I knew did. None of my friends, anyway. Third year. Third year was before Emma met Paul, before Sinéad threw herself into the world of romance. There were boys but no one had *sex* with them. If you did *anything* it was worthy of extensive analysis.

Now we don't talk about it, not in that way we used to. Maybe it's the change in the group, with no more Lisa and no more Emma and a half-reinvented Sinéad and a newfound Jen. Or maybe, I think for the first time, it's because we're past that stage of needing to analyse every single sexual act and get reassurance from our friends.

Maybe all my friends are having grown-up serious sexual relationships instead of the teenage melodramatic on-off going-out-together thing that I still thought, up until two seconds ago, was par for the course.

I can't believe *that* is what's going through my head right now.

"Do you know for definite?" I say, finally.

She shakes her head. "No. I found a test in the bin in our bathroom. Like, an hour ago."

"What, just sitting there for you to find?"

"No, it was down somewhere at the bottom. I was emptying the bin today, trying to be all responsible, and – yeah. A pregnancy test. With a line on it. And I don't know what that means, even, because I can't find the box and isn't there something about how one line just means it's working, or something? I don't know and I'm really going crazy here, Anna, I mean she's fifteen, for God's sake . . ."

"Breathe," I advise. "Where is it?"

"In the main bin, outside. I put it under all this other crap, I don't want the parents to see it. Though it's not like that's going to stop them from finding out. Oh God."

I decide not to go out and inspect. "Okay," I say. "If

it was down at the bottom, it's been there for a while. You're supposed to look at those tests within a few minutes, otherwise they don't give you an accurate result. And you don't even know if it was hers. It could have been one of her friends . . . you don't know. Just wait until she gets home, and ask her about it."

Lily is nodding. "Right. Right. Okay."

"Okay," I say.

She's calmer now. It's easy to be the calming force when you're still in shock about the whole thing.

Denise and Lily are the closest things I have to sisters, the cousins I'm closest to, the ones I grew up with. Penny and my mother were friends even before my parents got married. They can talk on the phone for hours, like kids. We're all part of a universe where teenagers go to school and sit exams and go off to college, where problems like this don't exist. I know that statistically there are teenagers out there getting pregnant. I just don't know where they are. They're somewhere else. Not in my family.

I want to believe that the test belongs to some friend of Denise's. Or that it's negative. But then I think about the facts of what Denise has been like lately – out all the time, not making an effort in school, completely devoted to her boyfriend – and put them together as though she's not someone I've known all her life. It matches up exactly with my idea of the kind of girl that gets pregnant as a teenager.

The kettle switches itself off and I make a pot of tea for us.

"Have you called her?" I ask Lily.

"She's turned her phone off. She's been doing that a lot lately. She'll probably be home around one or two. She's supposed to be in by eleven, but she's not good with that whole time concept." Lily's tapping her fingers on the table.

"It'll be fine," I say.

I want to believe that. I'm not sure I do. But it's all I can say or do for the moment.

I put on a pizza while Lily practises scales on the piano. She's been playing the piano for years, but scales are calming, apparently. I listen and remember being seven and trying to learn the recorder. I never made it past that stage, got to learn how to play a 'proper' instrument.

There are things I know I'll never succeed at. I wouldn't even be able to tell, right now, if Lily made a mistake and went off-key. I can't run fast. I can't speak in front of an audience; even discussions in class that require more than one-sentence contributions make me nervous. I am clearly not anything close to a social butterfly.

But listening to Lily play makes me wish that I

could do something else apart from school stuff, have something else that I'm good at.

I sit at the kitchen table and attempt the Sudoku in yesterday's paper while waiting for the pizza to be ready. I don't think this quite counts as a special skill.

Everything has to be okay with Denise. And even as I'm telling myself this, I'm listing off the options like a magazine agony aunt. Keep it. Give it up for adoption. Have an abortion. I try to remember what exactly the rule is about leaving the country for abortions, if you're officially supposed to pretend you're going abroad for some other reason. Vicky would know. Vicky's argued 'that this house would legalise abortion' or something like that – she gets the legal system.

I'm hopeless. What do people do, really? If Denise really does have a baby, what will she do with it? She's supposed to be doing exams, not – giving birth. It's ridiculous.

She's fifteen years old, for God's sake.

When the pizza's ready, we eat it in front of the television. Laughing at old sitcoms is familiar enough to make me feel safe. Life's the same as it's always been, it has to be. Everything's fine. We open a bottle of wine and flip through the guide to see if there's a good film on.

And then Denise gets home.

To Do List: Vicky

Xmas presents
Ask Rob re: 26/12
New top
Homework!

To Do List: Anna

Homework:
Maths (for J).
Chemistry (2005 Q4).
English (2003 essay).
French (vocabulary).

Reading:
Biology (chapter 18).

Notes:
Irish (poetry).
Biology (chapter 17).

Other:
Christmas presents.

21

Vicky

In the last week – three and a half days really, we finish up at a quarter past twelve on Thursday – in school before the Christmas holidays, I somehow manage to avoid handing in every piece of homework due in. Ms Black never takes our work up, of course, trusting us to put in the effort ourselves, so that's not a problem. I arrive in late on Tuesday morning and miss geography class again, the last one before the end of term. I stick my late slip inside the cover of my homework journal and look at it when sitting in English. It's thin and blue, with my name scrawled on the 'student' line and a red ink stamp with the school name and the date.

These things used to seem terrifying. The so-called

cool girls would walk into whatever class we had first thing in the morning, ten minutes after the teacher had started talking, and wave their blue slip in a bored fashion at the teacher before slumping into their seats. The elaborate boredom was the infuriating thing, the dramatic yawning or rolling of their eyes or whatever. Stupid girls.

Genuine apathy doesn't involve that much heavy sighing, or pen-clicking, or anything else. If you genuinely don't care, you don't feel the need to prove to everyone else in the class just how much you don't care. You can not-care quietly, while sitting with an open copy of *Macbeth* and a blue slip sticking out of your homework journal, because your English teacher has seen you debating and thinks you're great and doesn't bother giving you a stern look when you say that you left your essay at home because you're not one of the ones she needs to worry about. Mrs Mooney is teaching the top class in English. I think she thinks she doesn't need to worry about us, not in any real way.

There are twenty-seven in the class, including seven girls who have represented the school in debating and public speaking at some point, two who've done Olympiad stuff (Laura for maths, Martina for chemistry), two who got all A's in the Junior Cert, one who writes a column for the local newspaper, and an assortment of others in no danger whatsoever of coming anywhere near failing their English papers. Martina's known for bursting into tears every time she doesn't get a good enough mark, but her main worry is that she'll get an A2 instead of an A1.

No one bothers too much about comforting that kind of girl, in the same way that teachers don't worry too much if one of the 'good' students slips up a bit. It's so easy. Too easy.

It's almost Christmas. When January rolls around I'll get myself organised. Maybe.

I think about Rob and how he hasn't replied to my latest text message about coming over to my house on St Stephen's Day. It's a week away yet and I'll probably be seeing him before then but I assume that like most people he has family stuff on over the holidays. On Christmas Day we have the two sets of grandparents over, which usually involves a lot of tedious and depressing old-person talk about hip replacements and Biddy down the road who's passed away and how Mary hasn't been the same ever since her husband died and other such cheery topics. It's the only day of the year I'm grateful to have Tara in the same room as me, to raise eyebrows at over the table when the lamenting over whatever recently or not-so-recently deceased apparently lovely yet suspiciously distant relative they hadn't seen in forty years is going on. The Christmas two years ago I intended to stay in my room and avoid the whole thing but the parents talked me out of it. I didn't even get a proper rebellious being-fifteen moment there, I think, no wonder it's all catching up with me now.

Stephen's Day is when my parents have a couple of their friends over, and the aunt and uncle who don't talk to the grandparents and therefore will never come over on Christmas Day, and I sometimes invite a few of my friends over depending on what they're doing. This year I want to have Rob there, to introduce him to people, to just have him there next to me making conversation and being funny and being mine. I've tried to make it sound as casual as possible, not like I'm dragging him over to be interrogated by my entire family or anything like that. It's just another day of drinking and hanging out, nothing to get stressed out about.

We're supposed to be thinking about the issue of kingship in *Macbeth* and my mind is as per usual elsewhere, wondering if he even got my text or wondering if he's thinking up a way to get out of it without hurting my feelings or wondering whether he's just hopeless at getting back to people. My money is on the last option. But you'd still think that he'd make an effort with replying to someone he slept with a week and a half ago.

I mean, not that sex has to involve a lifelong

commitment or anything, but surely it implies at least some obligation when it comes to text messages?

I look at my late slip again. I'm the kind of girl who gets late slips now. I'm the kind of girl who has sex.

I know that in real life there's no sharp divide between the good girls who study lots and don't drink or sleep with boys or have any fun, and the bad girls who don't care and do whatever the hell they want. Anna drinks. Laura has a boyfriend. Jen's going to teach little kids when she grows up.

And last year in school, and last summer, I managed to be both someone who did well in school and didn't worry her parents too much and someone who went to parties and did 'everything but' with boys and I've never even believed in the whole idea that you keep your virginity until one specific act, like you're still chaste and sweet and innocent even when you're doing all that other stuff that's just as intimate.

It's not like I was 'saving myself' for Rob. What a ridiculous idea. It wasn't anything special because of that, it was special because it was me and Rob and I think he's amazing.

So why the fuck am I acting like someone who really does believe in the idea that sex is some mystical bond that you can't escape from?

I keep thinking about it all through the day. I wonder if it's because it really is that important to me or because once I get started on it, it's a lot more interesting a topic to focus on than important vocabulary words relating to the issue of homelessness (Irish), or listening to Laura asking an insightful question to do with integral calculus that makes Ms Black look as though she's discovered a future Fields medallist or something (maths class, what else?).

At lunch time Jen and I queue up to get hot water for our Pot Noodles while Sinéad and Anna are sitting down with their sandwiches, and I'm about to ask her whether she's been talking to Rob or not when she says, "Me and Luke broke up last night."

"Oh, Jesus. Are you okay?" I ask. Obvious, stupid question. I've had three classes with her today; how did I not pick up on something this huge?

She nods in that way that means she's very much not okay. "Don't mention it to anyone yet, ok? I don't want to talk about it yet."

I feel sorry for her but also selfishly disappointed that I can't really discuss my own stuff with her at the moment. I also hate the fact that I know there's nothing you can really say in these situations to make anyone feel better. The last relationship I had was really more of a summer fling, a month of drunken messing around at parties before he headed off to America and I went to France and we agreed that we weren't going to resume things when we both got back. But even that was upsetting enough, having been with someone who wasn't prepared to take a chance on me – I mean, of course I knew it was only a casual thing and it wasn't going to work out in the long term, but having it stated quite so bluntly by someone still hurts. You sort of hope they'll like you enough not to be weighed down by logical reasoning.

With Jen and Luke, I know there's no point in reminding her of how often she's been annoyed at something he's said, or how much time she's spent crying in bathrooms over him. Not yet.

The days slip by in school. The teachers give us homework for the holidays. I'm not thrilled. I can't believe everyone else just nods and accepts it. Why aren't they mutinying against this kind of thing? It's Christmas. What's wrong with them?

Rob finally gets back to me on Thursday. I leave my phone at home deliberately, on the unscientific but apparently accurate principle that he's more likely to text me at a time when I won't be able to read the message right away. He can't make it for Stephen's Day, sorry. That's what it's taken him three days to say? I go back and forth between disappointed and annoyed, still dancing between the two when Sinéad has us over for a girls' night in that evening. Despite not wanting to talk about her break-up with Luke, Jen's managed to tell everyone separately about the fact that it's happened. I find it ironic that it's Sinéad, she who has no guilt about abandoning us on nights out the instant Mr Right approaches, who's organising a get-together to prove that friends are better than boyfriends, but it's just what I need tonight.

Sinéad and Jen are mixing cocktails in the kitchen, while Anna and I sort through the DVD collection to find something appropriately girly to watch.

"This," I announce, "will be the chick flick pile." I've already added *Clueless, Legally Blonde* and *Mean Girls* to it.

"*Chick flick*?" Anna says. "I can't believe you just said that."

"What?"

She shrugs. "It's such a stupid name."

I don't dwell on it. But I do look at her and remember years of telling each other secrets and understanding one another, and how she's the only person in the world I want knowing that what happened with me and Rob was a first time. I don't want to make a fuss about it with him, or with Jen, or anyone else. I am cool Vicky.

"Hey," I say, in a low voice. "Can I tell you something?"

"Sure," she says. "Everything ok?"

"Me and Rob – after the Excuse Party – we, you know. *You know*."

"Had sex," she says.

"Yeah."

"If you can't even say it, you shouldn't be having it," she says, sounding like a hopelessly out-of-touch agony aunt. I watch her to see if she's joking. I don't think she is.

"Fine, we had sex." I wait for her response.

"Did you use a condom?"

Seriously. That's the question she's asking me. I regret ever bringing this up.

"Forget it," I say, "I don't want to talk about this with you. I shouldn't have said anything."

"You didn't, did you? What the *fuck*, Vicky?"

It's our sixth year in school together and it's the first time I've ever heard her swear. I'm not sure exactly what I've done that merits a reaction this strong.

"It's none of your business," I say. "And – God, it's not like – it's not like some problem-page thing where you sit down and have a serious conversation about birth control. It just happens, and –"

"Oh, it just *happens*, and then you get knocked up or diseased or –"

"You don't get it! Oh, God, you just don't *get* it, because you live in this little world where you know everything and experience *nothing* and –"

"And you seem to be living in a bubble, Vicky. You think – you think everything's just going to be magically okay, and it's not. That's not how the world works."

"Oh, like you have *any* idea about how the world works. You're so naïve –"

"*I'm* naïve? You're the one –"

"Hey!" And that's Jen, coming back into the room with Sinéad trailing behind her. "Guys. What's going on?"

She's going to be a great teacher. I feel like a five-year-old who knows she's been caught doing something wrong.

"Nothing," I say.

Anna stays quiet.

"You okay?" Sinéad is asking Anna, not me. Why not me, I wonder. Like she's automatically assuming it's my fault, whatever it is.

"Yeah," she says. "I'm going to head home, though. I – yeah. See you later, guys. Have a good Christmas."

I can tell that she's struggling not to cry as Sinéad hugs her goodbye. Jen and I stay where we are. Let her cry. Getting lectured on sex by someone whose actual experience in the matter is completely non-existent and who then has the nerve to accuse you of living in a bubble? God. I'm angry. I am so fucking angry.

I go into the kitchen, knock back a glassful of pina colada, and then feel my shoulders slump and the tears starting to fall.

22

Anna

I can't believe I'm walking home in tears for the second time in less than two weeks. I'm nearly eighteen and this is the kind of thing that's supposed to happen when you're thirteen and all the girls in school are total bitches and won't let you past them to get to your locker but then try to copy your science test two days later. I'm going to be in college in less than a year. I shouldn't be crying like a little girl.

But then again, I – what was it she said? *Know everything and experience nothing.* I am naïve and out of touch with the real world, according to Vicky. Like she has any right to – but does she really think that? Does she really think I'm like that or was she just lashing out because she knows I'm right, that she's being an idiot having unprotected sex with Rob?

Everyone in the world really is having mature, grown-up sexual relationships except me. Even if they're being stupid about them, they're still having them.

Even if they're getting pregnant at fifteen from them.

I keep seeing Vicky's face looking the way Denise looked that night she came home and Lily and I asked her what was going on. Scared and helpless and realising that it was real. What it was going to mean.

How does Vicky have the nerve to act like I'm the naïve one? She's the one who doesn't realise what she's getting into. She could so easily ruin everything for herself. She thinks everything's going to be okay. Like it's all right to come into school late or not do her homework, slowly turning into someone like Emma who's going to finish school probably still going out with her boyfriend but with results that aren't going to get her anywhere. And Vicky's smart enough to know better.

Like if she wanted to do medicine, if she actually set her mind on something like that and put in the work, she wouldn't need to worry about it. She'd have it, no question. She wouldn't be panicking over what might happen if she doesn't get it, or dreaming about impossible exam papers, or – she'd be *fine.* And instead she's going around like she's trying to screw things up for herself.

I can't be friends with someone like that. Not this year. I can't be distracted by all that drama. This is the year my energy needs to be directed towards studying, not on arguing with my friends or watching them do stupid things.

When I get home, quietly turning the key so I can get upstairs and wash my face before my parents realise I'm upset over something, I take out my notebook. Six hundred points. Medicine.

Forget about Denise, forget about Vicky. You can't write "Sorry, I had a dramatic year" in your exams.

I can focus. I can do this. I can't let myself regret anything next August when the results are out. I can't put myself in the position of wishing I'd worked harder instead of getting caught up in all this other stuff.

I can see what really matters, even if the rest of them can't. I have to keep remembering that. It's going to get me through this.

After I've dried my eyes, I go downstairs and switch on the computer. I borrow Dad's credit card so I can pay for the form to go through. My list: medicine, medicine, medicine. I know the course codes off by heart at this stage but I double- and triple-check them anyway.

I fold up the print-out and stick it inside my notebook, black-and-white proof of my goals. My ambitions. What really counts.

23

Vicky

Christmas is boring. The topic of whether or not I'm worried about the exams and what I want to do in college keeps on coming up, and I almost miss the conversations about how tragic it is that Paddy is 'on his way out' or whatever it might be. I leave my schoolbag in my wardrobe unopened and don't worry about it. The exams are months away, and anyway I think I've resigned myself to the fact that I'm not the academic type. It's a pity it's taken me so long to realise it, but still.

At least I can be fun. Chris turns eighteen on New Year's Eve and has a big party, and I spend most of the night keeping the mood light, impersonating Mrs Fitzpatrick and other teachers at the school, and mock-debating with one of the guys over the merits of vodka versus gin. There's an underlying tension at the beginning of the night, because Luke's here and Jen's here and they're not talking to one another, and apparently Rob's not talking to Luke because of the whole thing and Chris thinks they shouldn't be taking sides which is why he invited them both, but it slides away with the laughing and the drinking, as midnight gets closer and closer.

"You're really great, you know," Chris says to me in the kitchen when I'm opening another carton of orange juice for mixing.

I beam at him. "I'm so not. But thanks."

Just as I am thinking how utterly lovely he is, and how glad I am to have got to know this crowd, he kisses me. Oh, dear.

"Ah, Chris," I say, disentangling myself, "I don't think we –"

"You sure?" he murmurs, his thumb tracing my collarbone. Shivery and nice. But he's not Rob.

"I'm sure," I say, and walk away before it gets messy. Where the hell is Rob, anyway? All I got from him earlier was a hug, before he disappeared to get a drink. Not that I'm expecting him to stay at my side all night long, but I think I deserve to at least get a chance to talk to him, for things to be the way they used to.

I step outside the front door, wondering if he's out here smoking, and instead find Chris's little sister, who's in Tara's year, sucking on the insides of her cheeks and looking pale.

"Hey, sweetie, are you okay?" I ask. It's always so much easier to be nice to other people's younger siblings.

She looks at me. "I think I had a little too much to drink," she says. She puts her hand to her mouth and swallows hard.

You don't say, I think but refrain from voicing aloud. It's not like I've never been sick on a night out. "You want some water?"

"I –" she begins, and then takes a moment before continuing, "I just want to go to bed, but my mom and dad are in there and I don't want them . . ."

I try to remember where I last saw Chris's parents. I leave the girl outside and check on them, then help her back inside and up the stairs before her parents wander out of their front room and see her. She falls into her bed and I leave a glass of water on her bedside table. I check around for something for her to get sick into if she needs it, but the upstairs bathroom's locked. I tap on it. No response.

I'm about to go downstairs again when the door opens, and Jen and Rob slink out.

I've had a few drinks tonight, but I am still sober

enough to help a fourteen-year-old kid upstairs. I am still sober enough to understand what's going on.

"Your top's on backwards," I say to Jen, and shove past her to get into the bathroom, where I find a bucket in the press. I don't look at either of them when I walk out, just leave it in Chris's sister's room for her, and then wander down the stairs like I'm on a slow-motion setting.

She's always said that nothing was ever going to happen between her and Rob ever again.

And she completely encouraged me to go for him. What was that all about?

And she's only just broken up with Luke. And he should know better than to go after someone just after that. I mean, even if he doesn't care about me – which, well, he clearly doesn't, and now everything's getting blurry.

I want someone to give me a hug and tell me everything will be ok. I want a friend. I want Jen except she's the problem and I want Anna except she's the other problem and I sit on the front steps and sniffle. Inside everyone is counting down to midnight.

I feel pathetic. And you'd think that someone would come out to check on me, someone like Jen or Rob to apologise and see if I'm all right, or even someone like Chris just because he's noticed I'm not there, but everyone inside is doing their own thing and no one cares.

I no longer feel pretty or interesting or desirable or cool or fun. I just want to go home. My bag is on my arm and I can pick up my coat some other time.

It'll take me half an hour to walk home. By the time I turn the corner I'm regretting leaving my coat behind. Maybe I should go back and get it. But I don't want to see those people again. Not now. Maybe not ever.

I keep walking. One of Alan's friends lives on this road – I went to a house party here a year or two ago. I wonder if that's the one with the guys sitting outside in the front and smoking. I hope I don't look like I've been almost-crying. I don't want the pitiful image of me walking home alone at five past midnight on New Year's to get back to anyone I know.

"Hey," one of the guys calls out. "Vicky!"

"Is that Alan's Vicky?" someone else says, a familiar voice. "Do join us, Victoria."

I walk over to him. "I'm not Alan's Vicky," I say to James, my hands on my hips.

"Whatever you say," he shrugs, like he knows better. I hate that smugness. And he looks like an idiot sitting out here smoking, far too like a twelve-year-old trying to be cool. "What are you doing here, anyway?"

"Just heading home," I say.

"Party?"

"Yeah."

"Bit early to be going home," he says.

"You don't say," I snap.

"Hey," he says, tugging on my hand and getting me to sit down next to him, suddenly being nice, "what happened? Are you okay?"

The thing is, I actually do really like James, at least some of the time. I know that he thinks I'm attractive, if nothing else. And I like that he's the first person tonight to ask me if I'm okay.

"I'm fine," I say, but I lean on his shoulder anyway.

Oh, screw it. He's cute, and I owe nothing to Anna or Rob or anyone else. I wait until he takes a swig of the beer in his hand before leaning in to kiss him. Happy New Year, James. Happy New Year, self.

24

Anna

When we get back to school I start spending lunch in the library, head bent over a book. Lunch is easy enough to handle. I go up there as soon as the bell rings, find a table in a corner, and start making notes or reading over a chapter of something. The library is home to several visitors finishing off homework before it's due in after lunch, or people cramming for tests, so I fit right in. No one can tell from looking at me that I'm planning for something bigger than just some twenty-minute test in my next biology class.

Six hundred points. There are over fifty-five thousand of us sitting the Leaving Cert this year, all over the country, and only a tiny percentage get six hundred points. Most will get in the three hundreds or four hundreds, maybe because that's all they're capable of or that's all they need for their course or that's all the work they're prepared to put in. It's the IQ bell-curve in a microcosm, with six hundred as the ceiling. It's designed to have most people clustered around the centre.

I am not going to be *most people*, and that's what keeps me going throughout these lunch times.

Every time I go to the toilet in school, and close the cubicle door behind me, I have a moment where it's tricky to breathe, like on Tuesday evenings before James is due over. Maybe it's the closed space that makes it all hit me. What if it doesn't work out, what if it all goes horribly wrong, what if, what if.

One chance. One set of exams. I think about James, getting through it no matter what happened. I think about Alan, the debating star turned repeat student. I think about how it has to all go well. It *has* to.

The morning break is harder. I sit at the back of a classroom, drinking coffee out of my thermos flask, and try to find something to occupy myself for those fifteen minutes. It's important, I know, to take advantage of every short period of time you have available to you. Not just hours at a time, but a few minutes here and there. That's how people get things done.

But a few rows ahead of me, Vicky perches on her

desk and talks to people, girls in the class who aren't good friends but who aren't not-friends either. Jessica, Ruth, Sandra. They talk about school and grinds and teachers and nights out and boys and television. Vicky's always been so good at talking to people, at having lots of casual friends.

My brain says: let her have that. Let her at it. She'll regret it when June rolls around, when August arrives.

I stare at the book in front of me and try to focus on that, try not to be quite so acutely aware that I'm sitting alone in a classroom filled with groups of people chatting and being friends and being normal.

I try to think Big Picture all the time, even in the middle of the minutiae of school. It doesn't matter that I don't have anyone to talk to about trivia.

I hear three versions of the story about why Jen and Vicky aren't talking, one of which even incorporates my own not-so-pleasant encounter with Vicky at Sinéad's thing, before Jen gives me her version in French class.

"She won't even tell me why she's not talking to me," Jen says, shrugging. "She's just – not. I don't know if it's about Rob, or something else . . ."

"What happened with Rob?" I ask.

"I think she's pissed off that he was spending so much time with me after me and Luke broke up. But he's one of my best friends, you know? And they weren't even going out, you know?" She sighs.

"Well, Vicky's kind of irrational sometimes," I say. I force myself to phrase it that way. Not to say that she's a bitch. Because if I said that, I am willing to bet that Jen would repeat it to Vicky at some point in the future. They'll be friends again, probably. They'll sort it out.

I have no interest in sorting anything out with Vicky, or puppy-doggishly asking Jen where she's hanging out at break now that she's not talking to Vicky, or starting a conversation with Sinéad when, despite being nice enough when I left her house, she hasn't spoken to me since then. I don't have any classes with her. And lunch is my library time, avoiding everyone.

My eighteenth birthday is at the end of January. Dad asks me the week before if I have anything special planned, but I say no, not with the mocks so close.

"You sure?" Mom asks, which I feel is not the sort of response to have to a daughter being sensible about exams.

"Yes, I'm sure," I sigh.

"Well, will we take you out to dinner, anyway?" Dad says hopefully, so I give in to this plan. They seem so set on celebrating it, like it means anything that I'm going to be eighteen. It's only technical adulthood. There's a whole load of girls in school who have already turned eighteen and they certainly don't act like real grown-ups all of a sudden.

What makes you an adult? It's definitely not having a birthday.

Penny, Noel, Denise and Lily join us for a dinner in a local restaurant three doors down from the Tiger Bar, which reminds me of the night of the Excuse Party as we pass by it. We haven't seen them since Christmas, but Lily and I are emailing constantly these days, my one indulgence when I'm figuring out how much internet time I'm allowed have. Denise told them a couple of weeks ago about the baby. They've had her talking to people to try to figure out what she wants to do, going to the doctor, all that. According to Lily, the most upsetting thing for Penny is that it's due at the same time as the exams, that it has to mess up her education in such a clear-cut way. She wants Denise to have the baby and then go back to school, not to let it interrupt her studies.

It's a subject we dance around at dinner. I know. I know Mom knows, because she and Penny have been having long phone conversations, and I can tell from the way she looks at Denise, and I presume Dad knows because Mom would have told him, or because Noel would have, but it's not something that anyone is saying out loud. This, like whatever is going on with Ian and Charlotte and Phil, is something that is never going to be openly discussed. These things, I am realising, do happen in families like ours. We just pretend they don't.

The grown-ups ask Lily how college is going, and me about whether I'm ready for my mocks, and maybe I should feel the weight of pretence on all of our shoulders, talking about irrelevant issues to distract us from the pregnant fifteen-year-old sitting across the table from me.

But instead all I can feel is how genuinely proud they are of the kids who are going to do well, the one who's going to get her degree, the one who's going to get into medicine and eventually be a doctor.

And that makes up for being in bed by eleven on the night of my eighteenth birthday, checking my phone one last time to see if Vicky or any of the others have remembered the date or cared about it before switching it off.

25

Vicky

Luke invites me to his eighteenth at the end of January. Sinéad's been invited too, but she declines because she's not going out until after the mocks.

"Ah, it's just one night," I say, trying to tempt her. She's the only one of my good friends I'm still talking to, even though we've never been especially close and I haven't spoken to her much in school since we came back after Christmas.

She shrugs. "Nah, I'm going to stay in. It's only Luke, anyway, I only know him through Jen and it's a bit weird if they're not together anymore."

I only know him through Jen, too, but I know some of the guys who'll be there, and it's a night out, something to do, something to plan an outfit for and think about and anticipate and then dissect when it's all over. But I understand all too well where Sinéad's coming from. Without one of my friends there, I don't really want to go either. One of the guys I know is Chris, and that'll be awkward, and I'd just end up drinking too much and doing something stupid, and I've promised myself after the thing with James at New Year's that I'm not going to go near any boys who only seem like a good idea when I've had a few drinks.

Someone else's birthday is around this time of the year. I remember on the Saturday night, the night that Luke's thing is on and I'm at home watching television and going online, probably because one of the things I'm doing tonight is filling out my CAO form before the deadline, that it's Anna's.

I wonder what she's doing to mark the occasion. Maybe a family thing. Maybe something with Jen and Laura and a few others from school. Maybe she's just studying. She's completely obsessed. In school she's always doing something, always working even during break time. It can't be healthy.

I miss her. Well, I miss Anna the way she used to be, when even if we disagreed we could still see each other's point of view. Before she became so incredibly judgemental.

It's the last year of school and even though I'm getting to know other people a lot better, talking to girls like Jessica and Sandra a lot more than even before, it's strange that it also means not having my old friends around. I never thought Anna would become someone like Emma who barely acknowledges me when we pass by one another in the corridors. I never thought Jen would, either, but then again I never thought she and Rob would ever get together and then not even bother apologising when I found out about it.

I check Anna's profile and notice that no one's left her birthday wishes. Not that she has many people added as her friends or even uses this thing all that much, but still. I'd feel guilty for smiling if she hadn't decided to lecture me on safe sex. I'm not pregnant and it's not like Rob is some sleazy disease-carrying fiend because, well, I'd *know*, I'm not an idiot. All I wanted was to talk about something important and she had to turn it into showing off how smart she is.

And she's not, she's not at all. I mean, she'll do very well in her exams, because she studies so hard, but that's meaningless in the end. If you work that hard of course you're going to do well, but it doesn't mean that you're smart. It doesn't mean anything.

It's just a set of exams. That's it.

I can see beyond it, to the real world. It's a pity that she can't. She's in for a real shock when she leaves school.

I switch back to the window with the CAO website. I stick down a couple of umbrella courses – general-entry science, general-entry arts – on my form, knowing that once I have something down I can use the change-of-mind thing in the summer, and then I check on a couple of ongoing debates in my favourite forum, adding a contribution to a thread on the purpose of the mock exams. I probably should start getting ready for them, but it's not like they really tell you anything about how you're going to do in the real thing anyway. We haven't finished the course in any of our subjects yet, although Ms Black, with her high expectations, has set out a plan for us which will leave us with a month for revision at the end of the year.

I am not in the least bit prepared. Jessica and I were talking about it this week, but she's one of those people addicted to telling others that they're going to be fine while going on about how completely screwed she is. I bet she'll do okay. Me, on the other hand – it's a whole other story.

But they're only the mocks, and I'm not the smart type, not anymore. That's okay. I'm coping with it. I can face up to the truth.

26

Anna

"So your mocks are next week, right?" James asks, looking up from a mess of papers. "When's maths?"

"Um, Wednesday, I think," I say. Actually, I know it's Wednesday, which also happens to be Valentine's Day, which I find very appropriate. Around James, though, I seem to turn into someone who isn't sure of these things, who doesn't know all that much. Maybe it's to do with the fact that I'm so hopeless in his specialty.

"Both papers in the same day?"

"Yeah. I know, it's stupid, that's not how they do it in the real thing, but . . ."

"Ah, they're only the mocks," he says, which has been the chant around school for the last week or so.

"So I won't see you for the next two weeks, and then is it mid-term or something?"

"Yeah, it is."

"Well, as fun as this is, and all, I'm pretty sure you'll want to leave it 'til the next week to start back?"

I giggle. "Um, yeah, that's fine."

He takes out his phone, puts the date into his calendar. "Cool. Okay, anything in particular you want me to go over before your mocks?"

I want to say something flirty like, *'Just me'*, and toss my hair at him or something, but instead I just shrug. I am not a flirt. I am my usual boring self, with an additional layer of tiredness. Getting ready for the mocks has taken over my life. Sure, they're 'only' the mocks, but they're the best indicator of how ready you are for the real thing. Most of the tests in school at this point consist of a few questions taken from past papers, but they're not the paper in its entirety, under real exam conditions instead of school test conditions, where the desks are close enough for people to copy or whisper to one another. The mocks are where you figure out what you need to work on, not just what material you need to revise more thoroughly but also what test-taking skills you need to improve, like reading the questions properly and not missing out on anything, or dividing your time between questions.

To be honest, there's a really big part of me that can't wait to sit them. I'd rather just go into school now and start frantically writing, instead of waiting for it. I'm not in the mood for playing about with mathematical concepts tonight, even if it is with James. I want to be tested by the exam paper, not by him.

"Okay, then we'll take a look over logs," he says.

"Do we *have* to?" I sigh. It comes out much more ditzy-girlish than I imagined. I must sound like such an idiot, and it's not as though he has any belief in my intelligence anyway.

He grins at me and says, "Yeah, we have to." His voice is warm and he's looking at me like he's seeing me for the first time.

I'm fizzing inside. "You're such a spoilsport," I say, suddenly finding it easy to be flirtatious.

He just laughs. "Come on, we're going to get some work done. And then if you're good, you might even get a break."

He starts explaining something but I don't hear him. The fizzing peters out and I try to figure out why. Things were going so well, and there was a definite something, and then – and then – it just stopped. Because he didn't give in and just start kissing me, or something? No, that's not what I wanted.

If you're good, you might even get a break. The tone.

Still flirtatious, but also – something else. There was some other dimension to it. *If you're good . . .*

Like I'm a kid. Joking, and friendly, but still – playing up the fact that he's nominally the one in charge in that way isn't flirtatious. It doesn't work for me. Being treated like I'm so much younger, like he's so much older and wiser and *better* –

I look at him, look at his magical hair and follow the way his mouth opens and closes as he talks to me – no, *at* me, I think – and it's like he's punched me. He likes this, that I'm the stupid one, the idiot in this situation. The more ditzy I seem, the more he likes me.

I don't hear a word he says until he's gathering up his things and wishing me good luck in my mocks.

It's not about luck, I snap at him inside my head, but I just nod and smile and thank him anyway.

And then I sit back down at the desk and try figuring out logs for myself.

27

Vicky

The Saturday night before the mocks start, I'm at Alan's house along with Colm and Niall, a couple of his repeat-buddies, none of whom are sitting mock exams this time around and therefore haven't turned into the study-obsessed freaks that everyone in school seems to have become this past week.

I mean, really, it's Saturday night. They're not studying on Saturday night. They're watching television or they're online or they're texting their boyfriends or something. No one could possibly sit down with books and notes and past papers at ten p.m. on a Saturday.

My parents seem to believe that that's what I should be doing, though, which is completely ridiculous and just shows how totally out-of-touch they are with how people's brains actually work. The only reason I'm allowed out of the house – 'allowed' being a fairly nebulous term for the tight-lipped "just don't stay out too late" I got while leaving – is because they think Alan's trustworthy and reliable and all those other good things that apparently their own daughter isn't.

"So, mocks starting on Monday, right?" Alan says to me, as bad as the parents.

"Yeah," I say, rolling my eyes and opening another can of beer, yanking the ring-pull thing back and forwards as I go through the alphabet.

"What'd you get?" Niall asks, clearly familiar with the ways of women and the mystical powers of cans in determining one's true love.

"J." I toss it on the table. I think not, somehow.

"James," Alan says unhelpfully. He seems to have a knack for saying exactly what I don't want to hear tonight.

"He's not my type," I say truthfully.

Alan looks at me knowingly but wisely says nothing. I presume he knows. Boys talk. That's fine. It was just one kiss and it doesn't mean anything. Not like I slept with him or anything. Jesus.

"How's Anna doing?" he asks instead. "Is she stressing out?"

I shrug. "I assume she is. I haven't been talking to her."

Niall and Colm are conducting a conversation about the latest games console and the cheapest place to get it. Alan frowns at me. "Why not, what's going on?"

"I don't really want to talk about it," I say, which is actually a huge lie. I do want to talk about it. I keep having arguments with Anna in my head about her approach to exams, to boys, to life in general. I just don't want to explain to Alan what the actual fight was about, because he'd get caught up in the nit-picky details about me and Rob instead of how the fight completely illustrates exactly why we just can't be friends anymore. I sort of suspect he'd give me a lecture on safe sex too, and that's just so very much not the issue here.

"Did something happen? Did she steal your boyfriend or something?" He's kidding about the second part, but genuinely interested.

"No, that was Jen. And don't get me started on that, either. Look, the thing with Anna is just – like, she thinks she knows everything. And then she tells you. And it's just really fucking annoying."

I wait for his response. He looks as though he's trying not to laugh. "Oh, come on, Vicky," he finally says. "Thinks she knows everything? Does that sound like anyone else we know?"

I look at him. "No," I say, genuinely confused. Why is he going off-topic like this?

He leans back on the couch. "I remember," he says in an avuncular fashion, "a certain debate I did back in the day."

'Back in the day' was only a few years ago, I'm tempted to say, but hold back.

"I don't even remember what it was about, it was something about immigration, I think . . . and this little pipsqueak stuck her hand up when they opened it up to the floor and criticised not only every point that I'd made, but then picked on the other team for not having made those criticisms during the debate." He laughs. "And then I got best speaker."

I laugh too. "You deserved it. You were great."

"But."

"But I still think I made some valid points."

"You did. Mostly. You brought up some stuff that we'd deliberately decided not to cover because it wasn't directly relevant, but yeah, you made a lot of good points. When someone on the team said you'd been there for the Juniors, we decided you were clearly some genetic experiment put into the mix to make all of us feel bad or keep us on our toes or something."

I crack up. "Yeah, that's me. That'd explain a lot."

"But – you see what I mean, right?"

I shake my head. "No. I don't. That wasn't me thinking I knew everything. That was me speaking up on a certain issue I happened to know certain things about. It's totally different."

"Is it?"

"Yeah," I say irritably. "There's a lot I don't know, Alan, and I *know* that, okay? There's a lot I know nothing about, including most of what's on the Leaving Cert syllabus, for God's sake."

He laughs, short and sharp. "Oh, drop it, Vicky. Stop fishing. Please."

"I'm not," I say, and he's still just shaking his head in that patronising way. "I'm not," I repeat, and then I put down my can.

"Hey, Vicky, I'm going out for a smoke, wanna come?" I can't tell if Colm's picked up on the tension or whether he's just being friendly.

"Sure," I say, and I accompany him outside into the February cold, taking a new can with me. I am Vicky, friend to smokers, even though I haven't touched a cigarette since I was eleven, my first and only hands-on experience with the things. I don't like leaving people alone, though, or missing out on conversations that happen in smokers' corners.

Tonight I'm bad company, though. I sit in silence, refuse Colm's offer of a cigarette, and think about what Alan's said in between gulps.

I was *not* fishing for compliments. I was trying to defend myself from him accusing me of being some sort of arrogant brat, not demanding that he step in and stop me from berating myself and tell me that I'm actually smart and brilliant and wonderful.

I wouldn't have believed him if he did. I know I'm not those things.

The truth: when that 'little pipsqueak', as Alan so eloquently put it, raised her hand at the end of that debate, she was trying to show off. Oh, sure, she believed what she was saying, and she did think that the guy's speech would have been better if he'd taken these things into account, but it was a debate, she didn't want to attack him personally. She wanted to impress him. Not because she thought he was cute or anything, but because she thought he was amazingly smart and so confident and completely deserved his best speaker award and every prize he got after that. She wanted him to think that she could maybe one day be as good as he was.

And now he just thinks I'm one of those annoying girls who insist they're going to fail everything but never do. Like Martina. Now he thinks I'm waiting for someone to reassure me, instead of stating a fact that I am completely sure of.

Even if I am smart, whatever that means, it's not

the kind of smart that's going to make any difference in these exams.

Alan's one of the smartest people I know, and he dropped out of college. Alan knows exactly what he wants to do with his life, and he's supposed to be well on his way to getting that now, not stuck at this point with us, even if he's trying to play the wise-old-mentor role while he's here.

"Sure you don't want one?" Colm offers, holding out the pack of cigarettes in my direction.

"Nah, I'm fine," I say.

"So, why *are* you hanging out with us tonight instead of at home being a good student? You into Alan?"

"Nooooo," I say, drawing out the syllable. "We're just friends. And," I add before Colm can say it, "I know, I know, that's what everyone says and they usually end up hooking up anyway. But me and Alan, not going to happen. Well, it might, but it'd be one of those stupid drunk things that we'd both really regret, you know?"

Colm grins. "That's honesty, that is. Do you do these stupid drunk things often?"

His hair reminds me a little of Rob's. "I try not to," I say, somehow already slipping into stupid-drunk-things mode. The way he's looking at me . . .

"Look," I say, decisively, "are you flirting with me?"

"Em," he says. "Well. Yeah." He's half-sheepish, half-full of bravado.

"Why? Because I'm the only girl here tonight?" I am genuinely curious.

"No, because – I don't know, you seem interesting. And you're – you know. Hot."

I don't hear that often enough to be offended by it. "Really," I say.

"Yeah. Ah, come on, Vicky, you must have loads of guys after you, why're you picking on me?" He's smiling.

"I don't," I say, "I really don't. And I'm not fishing for compliments, so you can shut up."

"I didn't say anything." He's still smiling. I haven't scared him off.

I'm not used to this, to boys liking me more than occasionally, to people meeting me once or twice and finding me not just interesting or 'intense' (well, if you're going to strike up a conversation with someone clearly stuck in debate-mode, of *course* you're going to think they're intense) but attractive. I'm not used to being the one with the power to say no instead of hoping desperately that someone likes me back.

There's an inevitability to the way Colm leans in

and kisses me, his smoky alcohol breath acceptable only because I've been drinking.

When we go back inside, only because it's cold out, Alan raises his eyebrows at me at the way Colm's holding my hand, but I simply smile back at him. Your friend thinks I'm hot, Alan. Your friend takes me seriously. Ha. What do you think of that, hey?

28

Anna

Experts say that you should study in an environment as close to test conditions as possible. For this they recommend a quiet room, with an uncluttered desk, free from all distractions.

Experts clearly need to check in on what an actual test environment is like. This is not absolute silence. This is nowhere near absolute silence.

Someone somewhere is clicking a pen. People should be shot for that sort of thing. There are bottles of water being opened, heavy sighs coming from some corners, some coughing and throat-clearing. Paper rustles. Pens are tapped against desks.

I finish my essay on the role of fate in *Macbeth* and start on the 'why would you recommend that

Heaney's work be included in an anthology for teenagers' question, regurgitating almost word-for-word chunks of the essay that Mrs Mooney gave me an A1 on. Did you know that his poetry tackles issues that are appropriately thought-provoking for today's adolescents in this ever-changing and violent world? Me neither. I don't believe a word of what I'm writing but I'm getting it down on paper anyway.

I couldn't sleep at all last night but now, fuelled by adrenaline and caffeine, I'm powering my way through the paper. This is where it all pays off, all the hard work. It worries me slightly that this paper is so straightforward. Not the best preparation for the real thing to get an easier paper.

The accounting one reassures me; they give us questions that include every possible tricky thing you could ever be asked to do, covering anything and everything that might ever come up on a real question. I love it.

I adore the mocks. They're almost relaxing, in a way. Instead of being in school all day and then going home to do homework and study, it's just a case of coming in, emptying your brain onto the page, and going home. For two weeks I can legitimately just look over a few notes and then do appropriately restful things in the evenings. I get through an entire season of *Scrubs* the first week.

Inevitably, James keeps popping into my head when I'm sitting the two maths papers, but I poke him away and just focus on answering the questions. The thing is, though, despite my epiphany about his attitude towards me, or maybe other people in general, his face keeps appearing in my mind. Apparently there's a still little bit of fizziness that hasn't been stamped out.

I watch Vicky leave the biology exam early and order myself not to care or to be influenced by this in any way. Let her at it. She might be doing it this time because she can't answer any of the questions. I'm just going to concentrate on me.

"How's it going for you?" Jen and Sinéad ask me at separate times during the fortnight of mock exams.

"Okay," I say, shrugging. "You know."

You're not supposed to ever admit if you're pleased with how an exam went. It's asking for trouble. I don't say anything too positive about any of them. It's not like it means anything if they go well. The marks go on your report card, not to the CAO. You're not supposed to confess to anything more than an exam being not as bad as you thought it was going to be.

I hear the conversations going on after every exam as I gather up my stuff.

". . . I so know I messed that one up . . ."

"... that was impossible, ohmygod ..."

"... what did you get for number four? Is that even on our course?"

"... I did the letter one, I know I made loads of mistakes though ..."

"... I didn't have a clue about that one ..."

"... so not looking forward to getting that back ..."

I don't say anything, but I'm so tempted to scream at them and tell them to stop it, first of all because post-mortems like that are the least helpful things in the world, and secondly because they don't really mean it.

I just keep walking. I don't engage. I don't look back. I just keep going.

29

Vicky

We get our mock results back one by one, starting the second week back after the mid-term break. March, three months to go, and our English class is sickened by the fact that Martina got an A1 in the mock.

"Well," Mrs Mooney says to her, "at least we can be sure you're not going to fail the real thing!"

Some of us laugh at this for the wrong reason: Martina will still be a drama queen during the exams, the way she was during the mocks.

I can't help it. Even though we're not speaking, I'm desperately curious. "How'd you do?" I ask Anna when the class ends and everyone's heading off to lunch.

"None of your business," she says, tightening her grasp on her pile of books.

Well. That's that, then. I was making an effort. If she wants to be like that – fine. Whatever. It couldn't have been an A1, anyway, otherwise Mrs Mooney would have mentioned her mark along with Martina's.

"How'd you get on?" Sinéad asks me at lunch when everyone's sharing their results so far, everyone except Anna, who I haven't seen at lunch since – I can't even remember. There's a big group of us at the table, Jen included, even though in situations like this I just avoid speaking to her directly. It usually works out ok.

"Fine," I shrug. Three back so far. Biology, Irish, English. Low Bs. No disasters. No major triumphs. I don't know what to think.

"How'd you do in English?" Sandra asks Jen.

"72," she says.

"That's really good!" Sandra says in that way that certain people have. I can hear Anna in my head: *That's really good! Oh, look, you put your shoes on the right feet! That's really good!*

"I got 74," she continues before anyone else asks.

I got 74. That's depressing. I've never thought of myself as being on a Sandra-level of smartness. Not that she's an idiot, just that she's never been particularly academically inclined.

But then I'm not either, right?

On Tuesday French and Geography come back.

More Bs. Martina gets an A1 in her geography paper. I hear from Jessica, who's in the same class, that Anna got an A1 in accounting, and that their teacher won't admit the paper was too hard because if one student can do that well surely all of them should be able to.

"It's not fair to compare us to *Anna,*" she says to us at lunch, sighing.

"Anna's really smart," Sinéad nods.

"What's she going for, pharmacy, is it?"

"Medicine," Sandra says.

"She'll get it," Jen says.

I keep eating my Pot Noodle until the subject changes. I don't argue about whether she's smart or she isn't. It'd just sound bitter or something.

There's a few of the exams that take forever and a day to come back. "I'm sorry, girls," Ms Black says to us on the Friday, looking about as pissed-off about something school-related as teachers are allowed to, "but there's been some problem with a batch of them, and that includes your maths papers."

"But surely all they have to do is follow the marking scheme," Laura says, "it can't take that long."

"Longer than you'd think," Ms Black says sharply, and I am secretly thrilled that Laura has said something not-perfect to her. "Anyway, that's not the problem. I don't know what it is, they've probably spilled coffee over them or something."

I love it when teachers are cranky about this kind of thing. It's like when Ms Hollowell used to bitch about how the principal never sorts out debate stuff in time but then still takes all the credit when it goes well and the school looks good.

"Maybe you should just mark them next time," I say, and then worry that it sounds critical rather than sympathetic. Fortunately, she smiles.

"I think, Vicky, that that is exactly what I'm going to have to do," she says. "Okay. Right. Let's have a look at sequences and series, then, since we can't benefit from actually having your mock papers with us . . ."

I am glowing inside. Apparently I haven't quite managed to squash the former teacher's pet within. I am pathetic.

The sequences and series stuff suits me. For the first time since September I'm not spending maths classes finding the desktop utterly absorbing. Some of it is the standard sticking-it-into-the-formula stuff, but some of it is just about finding patterns, just seeing things, just understanding it. I *get* it. Why doesn't the rest of the course click for me the way this portion of it does, effortlessly sliding into place? This is how it should be.

"It's just not working out for me," Jessica says in frustration in a class the following week, when we're still waiting for our papers to re-emerge from wherever they are.

"You have to keep at it," Ms Black says, taking a look over her shoulder. "Just practice. It's all you can do. Here, there was an interesting one in the exams a few years back . . ." She starts flipping through her set of past papers, and we end up with two exam questions to 'take a look at' tonight.

I don't want to practise. I don't need to practise these, anyway. If you're good at something, you shouldn't need to work that hard at it, right? Isn't that how it works?

The rest of the mocks finally come back at the start of April. This is the point of the year, I always imagined, where I would simply need to revise everything, because I'd have devoted myself to each and every one of my subjects so whole-heartedly throughout the year. Instead I have a colour-coded study plan that I designed on the computer while conducting an instant-message conversation with Ruth about what she was going to wear to her eighteenth. And that's about it.

Sometimes I think that I'm just not capable of believing this is actually sixth year. Surely if it were really this close to the Leaving Cert, that part of my brain would have kicked in, better late than never, and forced me to do some work. If I were really in trouble, I'd have sorted myself out by now.

But I'm not. I get my physics and maths papers

back. A2 in physics. B1 in maths, and Ms Black calls me up to her desk to point out some of the mistakes I'm making with the part c's of questions. Somehow I've managed to fake my way through the majority of the questions, or just put numbers into the most obvious formula and had it work out for me.

Somehow I have a set of mock results on my report card that my parents can't complain about. And I know that it's not hard work, because hard work has nothing to do with this. I should be thrilled, really. I should be delighted. I should be patting myself on the back for getting away with doing nothing but going to parties and wasting time and kissing random boys and instead I just feel empty.

Decent, respectable results. Average – no, not even average. Good, but averagely good. Vaguely good. No dramatic failures anywhere to be seen.

"If you keep working hard," Mrs Fitzpatrick says to me – this being sixth year, we have to suffer above and beyond the usual call of duty and the one annual visit to her office – "you'll have nothing to worry about. You should be able to get almost any course you want. What is it you want to do again?"

"Well," I say, and then stop.

"Sorry, what was that?"

"Nothing," I say, shaking my head. "Nothing."

30

Anna

I'm still on the phone with Lily when the doorbell rings. I look at my watch and walk-and-talk my way downstairs. "Hey, that's me, it's my maths grinds guy," I say to her as I open the front door.

"Happy grinding," she laughs, and I can feel my cheeks getting hot as James walks in.

"Bye," I say, "I'll talk to you soon, okay?"

"Cool. Bye."

"Sorry about that," I say to James as we resume our usual positions in the spare room.

He just shrugs. I decide not to elaborate and explain that I didn't have time to get myself into my usual flustered state because I was talking to Lily about how Denise is getting on. She's getting big now, looking properly pregnant. Her principal, who sounds about as uptight as ours, 'had a word' with Penny about taking her out of school. I'm not sure they're allowed actually kick her out but Penny's already organised Denise to start at a different school in September, and had a few sharp words herself with the principal about her prioritising of the school's reputation over a student's education.

This is what's distracting me now, not James. He explains something to me and I'm off in a completely different universe.

"Sorry," I say, "I was – sorry. Can you go over that one more time?" He looks as though he's really making an effort to be patient, so I add, "I know, I'm sure this must seem really basic to you . . ."

"Well, yeah," he says.

Wrong answer, James. Wrong answer and you have stupid, stupid hair.

I decide not to mention that the higher-level maths mock papers finally came back to the school last week, and that I got a B1. 82. Highest in my class. I was talking to Sinéad after an assembly we had last week about organising our graduation stuff, which is ages away yet, and she said that no one in her class did exceptionally well either. A lot of marks in the 80s. Laura got 88, Sinéad got 81, Vicky got 84.

I do my homework, I pay attention, I get grinds,

and she's still doing better than me. I'd suspect her of being a secret studier, one of those girls who claims to have done nothing but spends hours every night frantically working, but I don't see where she'd get the time. In the snippets I hear of the conversations over break, she seems to be going out just as much as ever.

Two months left. I can't worry about her. Vicky doesn't need to be worried about. Not when it comes to her exams, anyway. She *is* just one of those people that everything turns out ok for. She can somehow be good at school and at a million other different things on top of that.

When we take a break from the joys of probability, James pulls out his phone and appears to be competing in some sort of a textathon.

"Girlfriend?" I ask, finding it easier to say things like this to him when his hair no longer has magical powers.

He grins at me like we're friends or something. "Yeah. She's amazing."

"That's not the girl – the one who came over on the open day, is it?" I ask.

He looks at me, puzzled, and then, "Oh, Emily? No, no. It's a girl from my course."

"Ah," I say, feeling embarrassed for remembering this detail from his life more clearly than he did. It's hard to forget everything about an obsession.

"Listen, don't mention it to Vicky, all right?" he

says earnestly. "Obviously she'll find out eventually, but I don't want it distracting her from her exams or anything, you know?"

"Sure," I say. Dazed. Totally dazed. Vicky? Vicky and James?

I excuse myself from the room for a moment, press my hand against my mouth, and laugh silently, hysterically. Vicky and James. Huh. Wow.

The next week is our last session before the Easter holidays. "Hey," I say to him, "I think this might actually be our last one – when I get back to school it's nearly May, and I know we only agreed up until early May anyway, and I know you have exams and everything, so –"

"Aw, Anna," he says, and he does look genuinely sad, "you should've warned me. We could've had champagne, or something."

"Yeah, that'd be really conducive to understanding Leaving Cert maths, wouldn't it?" I laugh.

He sighs. "I can't believe it's our last one."

I consider, for a moment, suggesting that we abandon the original plan, that he keep coming all through May even though now is the time for me to be revising everything, not learning anything new. But only for a moment.

"Ah, you've got your own exams to worry about," I say, "and I'll be fine."

"Yeah, you'll do great," he says, apparently meaning it.

I get one hug and a "Sure I'll probably see you around sometime" as a goodbye. He gives good hugs. As I watch him go I admit to being a little bit jealous of Vicky and whatever the two of them had.

I wonder if she's slept with him, too. That's a thought that isn't so funny, but I force it out of my mind.

I spend the first day of my Easter holidays figuring out exactly where I need to put in more work. My mock results worked out to five hundred and forty points. My worst mark was English, barely scraping a B3. My answers apparently lack conviction.

"What you need to do, Anna," Mrs Mooney said to me when I stayed back one day after class, "is write what you believe in, not what you think they want you to write. They're looking for evidence that you've thought about the texts, or the issue that you're writing about in the paper one essay, not just that you've learned something off."

To be honest it's not the first time Mrs Mooney has said something like that, but she's one of those teachers who's so enthusiastic about her subject that it doesn't necessarily translate into a good understanding of what the examiners are looking for. I've looked at the marking schemes. I know how their minds work.

But a B3. Ouch. The only possible way to drag that up to an A1 for the real thing is to do something drastic. And I thought the paper was so straightforward, too. Now I understand why no one ever admits these thoughts. In case they're proven horribly wrong.

A1s in biology and chemistry, the two subjects that are actually relevant to what I want to do. I sigh and stare at the papers for a moment. I need to keep working in those subjects, and not let them slide just because the mocks went all right. The worst thing in the world would be to do worse in the actual Leaving Cert. And then I need to work on the other subjects to get them up to A1 standard, and –

I'm just so *tired.*

I take a break and let time slip by online. I log in to a couple of sites and realise that for people like Vicky and Jen and Sinéad there's so much evidence that they've had a good year. I look at the pictures of the Excuse Party. I am in the corner of one of them, turned away rather than posing. There are so many drinking sessions, so many eighteenths. I look through some of the photos, half-recognising some of the faces. Jen's friends, who I can identify collectively if not individually. Girls from school and their boyfriends. I find none of Vicky and James together, or no evidence that anything serious ever existed between them. Going back far enough I can find comments left for one another on Vicky and Rob's profiles, but no sign of any in-joke-saturated messages between Vicky and James. He's chosen not to fill in whether he's in a relationship or not on his own profile, though, even though he's in one now, so maybe he just doesn't believe in putting that kind of stuff online.

I look through his photos, which go back a couple of years. I find some of him from when he was in sixth year, looking young in his school uniform. His hair was shorter then, his glasses slipping down his nose. I wouldn't have been intimidated by him then, I think. I find Alan in some of these pictures, grinning for the camera. There are a few of parties and nights out and I find Vicky in one of these, seemingly arguing with Alan and some other guy, frozen mid-hand gesture.

"Anna?"

It's Mom. I jump as though she's caught me looking at pornography or something. "We're having dinner now," she says.

I close the window and switch off the computer. I'm not hungry.

Everyone is having real lives and I'm just watching theirs. I'm looking at websites to find out what the people who used to be my friends are doing with their time.

I try opening one of my books after dinner, but I just stare at the words at the page and take nothing in.

We go over to Penny and Noel's at Easter, and Denise really does look pregnant. It's too real to avoid now, that huge swelling. She makes me nervous. I don't know what to say. She's always been the baby, and now she's almost a mother.

"What's she going to do?" I ask Lily when we get a moment away from the others. Lily I can talk to.

"Keep it," Lily says, "and she's fighting with Mom about going back to school."

"She doesn't want to go back?"

"She wants to be a mother," Lily sighs. "She's such an idiot."

"Do you mind?" Denise is standing in the doorway, arms crossed. And for a second we're all kids again, Denise following us everywhere we go. "I'd rather have someone to love than do well in some stupid exams. You don't get to call me an idiot."

"But you're so young," I say to her softly.

She considers this for a minute. "Really? Hadn't noticed."

And then we're laughing, and Lily's looking on and shaking her head. "It's not funny. It really isn't."

I hug Denise tightly before I leave. "Hey. Good luck," I say.

"Thanks. You too."

"Hmm?"

"Your exams, you ditz," she says, laughing at me.

Oh. Right. Those.

All the way home, I wonder what she's going to call it.

To Do List: Vicky

Maths h/w
18th ?
Tidy room
START STUDYING

To Do List: Anna

Study.
More study.
Remember the days of having a life.
Ponder meaninglessness of own existence.
Mope.
Sleep.
Make new to-do list.

31

Vicky

"Hi, Vicky, how are you getting on?" Ms Hollowell stops me in the corridor the first day back after the Easter holidays.

"Grand," I say, nodding and smiling, glad that I am not *persona non grata* with her despite not getting involved in debating this year.

"Listen, we're trying to put the yearbook together, for the sixth years, and I was wondering if you'd be interested in helping out with that – I know you must be very busy, it's just this week, really, and then it goes to the printers. I don't want to put pressure on you . . ."

"No, it's fine," I say. I remember seeing what the sixth years last year put together, and I like the idea of helping to create something that has fewer appalling spelling mistakes.

What Ms Hollowell fails to mention, and what I don't realise until lunch time, when I'm sitting around the table with the others, is who else is involved with this.

To my left is Martina, which surprises me because I thought she'd have more important things to do with her time at this stage in the year, and beside her is Jen, who smiles tentatively at me when I arrive. To my right are Natalie and her friend Wendy, responsible mostly for photos, by which they mean as many photos of themselves and their friends as possible.

I really need to learn how to say no to things like this, I decide.

"Okay, I think we need to make sure we have pictures of everyone in it," I say, looking through the collection.

"I think we do," Wendy says, wide-eyed. Liar.

"We can handle the photos," Natalie says, "and you guys can do the other stuff."

"We've only got fifty pages," Martina says. "We need to sort out how much space your stuff is going to take up."

Natalie sighs heavily, as though this is none of her concern. "Can we not just put it all together at the end?"

"No, we need to sort it out now," I say.

"You're not in charge, Vicky," she snaps.

"Natalie, we really do need to figure this out now," Jen says.

Natalie rolls her eyes and gets up. For one glorious moment I think she's going to abandon it entirely and let us get to work, but she's only getting something. Last year's yearbook. "This has ten pages that are just photos, and then most of the other pages have at least one photo on them. I don't know how we're going to make this work. We need to sort out what else is going to be in it first."

I start making a list. "Okay. Stuff we've done during the year. Stuff the prefects have organised, any sixth-year activities –"

"The table quiz," Martina contributes.

"Pre-Debs," Wendy says.

"Excuse Party," Jen offers.

Natalie shakes her head. "That's not a school event, we're not putting it in there."

Here we go.

We end up getting most of our work done in the rushed five minutes before the bell goes and lunch is over.

"I want to kill her," Martina says, half under her breath, when Natalie and Wendy leave.

Jen laughs. "Don't we all?"

"See you later," Martina nods to both of us.

I'm still gathering up all our bits and pieces, the lists and the yearbooks from previous years. I can feel Jen still in the room.

"Hey," she says. "So, Natalie's super-fun, huh?"

"Yeah," I say. "It's going to be –"

"Look, I'm sorry. I – I don't even really get what I did wrong, but for whatever it is, I'm sorry."

I have to stop myself from screaming. "You don't get what you did wrong? You hooked up with Rob! God. How could you not *get* that that's what it was?"

"But you and Rob were over! And it's not like I – lured him into bed or anything, he was just being really sweet to me when I was upset about breaking up with Luke, and things just happened, but – I mean, you know Rob, he's not really into doing the whole relationship thing . . ."

"I know," I say, "I know, but – we weren't over."

"I didn't know that," she says in a small voice. "Oh, Vicky. Fuck. I just – I mean, he said that the two of you had, you know, whatever, and the way he said it was like, okay, that's that done, it happened . . ."

"Yeah, but it wasn't like it wasn't ever going to happen again, you know? I mean he never said anything – I knew it wasn't a *relationship,* but it wasn't . . ." I trail off. I'm lost for words.

It never occurred to me that Rob and Jen didn't

apologise because they genuinely thought there was nothing to apologise for. Because it wasn't cheating on me, it was just – the two of them, happening.

I always knew Rob wasn't Mr Serious Commitment, that we weren't officially together, but I thought there was going to be more to us than just one night. I mean, there was flirting after that, there was still something . . .

"I really didn't think I was interfering in anything that was going on between you and Rob," Jen says earnestly. "I mean, if I'd thought –"

"No, I know," I say, interrupting her before she can continue.

She nods. "Are we okay? I hate not being friends with you, Vicky, it's been really hard." She sniffles.

"Oh, for God's sake, you're not crying, are you?" I say. Not meanly.

"Come on, we're nearly finished school *forever!* You must have a heart of stone."

"That's me," I say, hugging her before we go back to class.

I want to talk to someone about what an idiot I've been about the whole Rob thing, how utterly stupid it was of me to not realise that his lack of seriousness about *anything* would extend to me, even if he did like me.

It would be Anna, if she wasn't so judgemental

about the whole thing in the first place. She never liked him. Maybe she was right not to. I don't know.

I spend the whole week, and most of the next, because of course we don't get it finished on time, working on the yearbook stuff. There are quotes pages, lots of pieces about various things we've done over the past six years, a whole section entitled 'We'll always remember . . .' with contributions from about half the year. *We'll always remember . . . our first assembly . . . when a dog ran into the middle of our Science exam in second year . . . the trip to Glendalough! . . . Ms Hollowell's 'pep talks', we love ya . . . Mrs M and Mr K taking us to see 'Macbeth', you rock! . . . Garfield . . . Pot Noodle . . . the dancing priest . . . BOB! . . .*

They get more and more random as the list goes on, but I get most of the references. Six years. Six years and it's almost over. I'd be lying if I said I wasn't giving in to the nostalgia at least a little bit.

It does strike me as ridiculous to expect people to be able to deal with that, on top of the crazy exams.

The middle of May is right about the time people start fading away from school. We're on 'study leave' from the twenty-third on – our graduation is the twenty-second – but most of the teachers are just doing revision stuff now and so many people believe that they'll get more done at home. I wonder if they really do, or if they're just sitting around watching television all day. I suspect it's the latter.

I don't feel like I expected to feel this close to the exams. I'm not as prepared as I thought I would be, but I'm not overly worried either. I'm just – calm, I guess.

The middle of May is also when I turn eighteen, but since almost everyone has put their social lives on hold, barring our graduation thing, my parents take me to the pub down the road and buy me my first legal drink. Jen and Alan come along for a pint or two and we're all home safe and sound before midnight.

I try not to care about what a let-down it is, for my eighteenth, and start planning a bigger get-together to have during the summer, in that world beyond the exams.

But I hate it. I hate the way this exam has taken over people's lives in a way that nothing else ever has, how it makes even the most unenthusiastic of students start caring about what grades they're getting. I hate that it's everything. One shot. That's it. That's too much pressure for anyone.

I'm not ready for it. And I just can't believe it's almost here.

32

Anna

I feel the point of a graduation ceremony is somewhat lost when you have a system which requires students to sit exams after the school year ends. I don't want to be here.

I arrive with my parents, who seemed unable to comprehend why anyone would miss this unless they were dying, and reluctantly part from them. All the students have to sit together. I look around desperately for a friendly face.

I feel like the only girl in the entire year not part of some enthusiastically bonded group of friends, which logically I know can't be the case, but it really feels like it when wandering around trying to find somewhere to sit.

Jen appears at my left side. "Hey, Anna. We're sitting over there, you going to join us?"

"Uh," I say, oh-so-eloquently.

"Come on," she says, squeezing my arm.

I'm grateful for the inclusion and it comforts me when I see the assortment of girls sitting together. Not just a tight-knit group, but a loose gathering, where anyone might feel at ease. I sit in between Laura and Martina and when Vicky arrives she even smiles at me. I bet she's been totally sucked in by all this end-of-year end-of-school nonsense.

Our principal makes a speech, and then someone from the parents' association gets up there, and then Natalie, of all people, is apparently the one representing the students. Us.

Any cheery glow I might have had from having a group of decent, friendly people to sit with is dissipated when I see the photo montage she and Wendy have put together. Lots of smiling, happy people, and mostly the same smiling people over and over again. It purports to tell the story of how all of us, as a year, as a group, a team, whatever, started off as sweet little twelve-year-olds, and all grew up together into the mature eighteen-year-olds about to set off into the real world that we are today. Like we're all friends, like we've always all been friends, like everyone gets along and like it's always been wonderful and perfect. Like this last year has been some kind of exciting adventure instead of hard work and stress and lunch times alone and tears and –

I'm crying, and I'm crying for all the wrong reasons. This isn't how it was. It's all wrong.

"You okay?" Laura mouths at me, and I shake my head.

I manoeuvre my way past Laura and Sandra, and leave the hall by the side-entrance. The lights have been dimmed, and I don't think anyone apart from those two actually notices. Even from outside, I can hear lots of cheering and clapping and laughing as the photos keep flashing up. Green Day's 'Time of Your Life' is on repeat as the background music. It's so appropriate that no one seems to realise it's ironic.

I sit down on the ground and pull my knees up to my chest. There's no one out here. This side of the hall faces towards the sports field, far away from the car park and the rest of the school and the rest of the world.

I think about leaving, now, and just abandoning this stupid graduation thing. I can tell Mom and Dad I don't feel well, I think, and it's not like anyone's really going to miss me . . .

Yeah. I'll go. Once I'm able to stop bawling like a baby.

The door opens again, then closes.

"It's a stupid song, isn't it?" Vicky sits down next to me, leaning against the wall. I can sense her looking at me but I keep my eyes straight ahead. "Natalie picked it, of course."

"Of course," I manage to say.

She rests her head on my shoulder for a moment, then says, "Come on, make yourself look presentable, you've got to hear her speech."

I rub the sleeve of my school jumper across my face. I feel like a mess. Vicky pushes the door open slightly but I hold back. I don't want to go back in there.

She shrugs. "We'll hear it out here," she says, keeping the door ajar with her foot.

"I'm really just so honoured to be representing all of you at this graduation ceremony," Natalie says from the podium, dabbing ostentatiously at her eyes with a tissue. "It's just such an honour, really, guys. We've had a really good year, an amazing year, it's just been really, really good . . ."

"I knew that'd cheer you up," Vicky says, letting the door close.

"Oh my God," is all I can muster.

"I know."

"Oh my God!"

"I know!"

And we're laughing so hard that we need to lean against the wall for support.

"That took her two weeks to write," Vicky tells me. "*Two weeks.* Can you imagine?"

Jen slips out the door to join us. "Oh my God. That speech," she says. "Did you hear it?"

"Just the start," I say.

"It was enough," Vicky says.

"Oh, guys, you missed the part where she quoted, you know that song, the 'wear sunscreen' one?"

"Yeah, yeah."

"She had a bit from that, only she attributed it to Oscar Wilde. I kid you not."

We're practically shrieking by the time Sinéad steps outside. She grasps the situation instantly. "Bitches, the lot of you," she says. "It was a good speech. It was exactly what people wanted to hear tonight."

"Oscar Wilde, to my knowledge, never advised anyone on the wearing of sunscreen," Vicky says.

Sinéad winces. "Yeah, that was painful."

"And did you see the pictures?" Jen says. "She was supposed to get one of everyone in, but did you *see* them?"

"Not exactly representative," Vicky says, sighing.

"And the song," Sinéad adds. "Yeah, never mind, there's no point defending her."

We stand there for a minute before Jen says, "We should head back in. Don't want to miss out on my tea and coffee."

"I hope they have good biscuits," Sinéad muses.

And the four of us walk back into the hall.

Everyone's milling around the tables of tea and coffee, which is not worth trying to drink, or so experience of other school events has taught me.

The plan is to go home, get changed, and head out to some club, apparently. Jen's dad is playing taxi driver, so I am offered a lift.

At home I look in my wardrobe and try to find something club-appropriate. I haven't gone out in so long. I'm nervous, but it's all going to be okay; I don't have to walk in alone, I have a group. It's all going to be fine.

It's going to be at least one moment of sixth year that I'll remember fondly.

Nine o'clock rolls around and there's no sign of Jen, who said she'd see me at about a quarter to. I chew on my nails and wonder if it's all just a horrible joke, if they're all in the club already laughing at the idea of leaving me waiting at home alone. I tell myself that I'm being paranoid but it doesn't help.

My entire body relaxes when I see the car pull up outside. Five past nine. Twenty minutes late. I will not comment. I will just be grateful.

It's the kind of loud you need to scream over to be heard, suited to people who are happy just dancing and drinking. We buy our drinks – it being the middle of the week, they've a good deal on cocktails – and take them onto the dance floor. I dance for a while, awkwardly, wondering if this is what the entire night will be. Swaying back and forth to vaguely familiar music, self-conscious and unglamorous and wanting to be home in bed. For months I've been on a schedule, a satisfying routine of going to bed at eleven and falling asleep almost instantly and then finding myself capable of getting out of bed at seven a.m., ready and alert. I am not ready for the night to be only beginning now.

Everywhere I look I see girls from school, and a few of the teachers are out too, dancing away. The girls who never pay attention in school are the ones, apparently genuinely, cheering them on, dancing alongside them. It's a world gone mad in here. I don't belong in it.

While Vicky and Sinéad are debating the issue of whether or not to buy their maths teacher a drink, Jen gestures to indicate she's going out to smoke. "Wanna come?" she says in my ear.

I am not a smoker, but the idea of escaping the dance floor appeals to me. I follow her outside. We get our hands stamped as we leave, a blue smudge so that the bouncers don't need to waste energy remembering our faces.

"How are you doing?" she asks, lighting up.

I shrug. Tired. Awkward. Bored. "Okay."

"Good night, huh?"

"Yeah," I say, struggling to find things to say. "I can't believe the teachers came."

"Fair play to them," she says, inhaling, exhaling.

There's a few guys ahead of us when we move to go back inside, rummaging in their pockets for ID.

"I'm twenty next week," one of them says, "this is really depressing."

"Alan!" I say, and he turns around.

"Hey," he nods. "All graduated?"

"Yep. What are you guys doing here?"

"We finished up yesterday, didn't bother heading out, so Vicky told us to come along tonight."

"We're honorary girls," one of the other guys grins.

"Or in a really good position to pick up girls," Jen notes.

"Yeah, that was more the plan."

Age cards, passports, and stamped hands are waved at the bouncers and we head in together. Alan and I drift off towards the bar, while the other guys follow Jen to the dance floor. Vicky bestows hugs on them.

"See that guy," he says to me, "the one in the blue?"

"Right next to Vicky? Yeah. God, he looks very into her."

"He's besotted. They had a bit of thing a while back, before you guys did your mocks – that's really why he wanted to come tonight."

We lean against the bar and wait for our drinks. "So Vicky's had two of your friends, then," I say.

"Oh, yeah, the James thing. He's got a girlfriend now, though."

"Yeah, I know."

"You know, me and Vicky were always wondering if *you* and James were ever going to get together."

I look at him and laugh. The bartender puts our drinks down in front of us, another brightly coloured cocktail for me and a pint for Alan. I hand over a tenner and shake my head when Alan tries to give me money. "Get the next one, okay?" I take a sip. "Yeah, me and James. He is . . . pretty attractive. But he's so arrogant."

Alan says something I can't hear properly, and I have to lean in closer. "He's brilliant, though," he repeats.

"Yeah, but that's no excuse. I mean, Vicky's a total genius, and she's not like that."

"Yeah, but she does that, you know, that fake girly insecurity thing. Oh, I'm not smart at all, that crap."

I shrug. "I don't think she's that calculated, though."

"That what?"

"Calculated!" I say into his ear.

We end up taking our drinks outside, so that we can actually hear one another speak. The bouncers won't let us leave through the main entrance with them, so we go out through a side entrance that leads into an enclosed concrete yard. There are a cluster of smokers out here too, girls from school I never knew were smokers, have never seen in a social situation before. I wonder if they think Alan and I are more than friends. The idea appeals to me, these girls seeing me as someone who might have a boyfriend, who has a life outside of school.

"So, tell me," I say to Alan, "what's the deal with repeating just so you can do psychology? Like, you could've done it some other way and stayed in college. Through science or something. Or a post-grad course. Why go to all this trouble?"

He looks at me.

"I'm not criticising," I say quickly, "I'm just curious."

"Well," he says, "I just – wanted to do it my way, I suppose. Do the course I really want, not mess about with subjects I'm not interested in. And I didn't do my best in the Leaving the first time around, and –"

"Yeah. You want to do your best."

"Yeah."

I consider asking him what happens if your best isn't good enough, but I don't want to bring that up. But it hovers there, unsaid. "So, psychology," I say brightly. "Right, go on, analyse me."

He sighs heavily. "That's not what it's actually –"

"Yeah, yeah, I know, it's a scientific discipline which students should take only if they have a genuine interest in the social sciences and not simply because they want to figure out why they themselves are so screwed up." I grin.

"Have you memorised *every* course description?"

"Do you really want me to answer that?"

We're looking up at the stars, bonding over the fact that we've never actually done that thing where you look up at the stars and feel insignificant in a galaxy full of wonder, even though they are pretty, when my phone rings.

"Hey, where are you guys?" Vicky and lots of background noise.

"Outside, side entrance."

We are joined a few moments later by Vicky, the guy in the blue, Jen and Martina. As the others light up, Vicky leans in to me and Alan and says, "Oh, dear, what do I do?"

Alan feigns innocence. "With Colm? Well, when a man and a woman love each other very much . . ."

She pokes him. "Stop it. He's being really flirty and *nice* and I don't want to be *mean* . . ."

He sighs. "Fine. I'll protect you."

"My hero!" she says, patting him on the head.

I wonder if he likes her. Probably, if he's keeping tabs on who she's been with.

The tiredness hits me again, and I start the round of goodbyes. I'm too sleepy to even consider giving in to the chorus of 'ah, don't go yet!' I was here. I danced, I drank, I talked. It's enough. I did it.

33

Vicky

Up at the bar I decide to be sensible and get water instead of taking advantage of the cheap cocktails. I worry that Colm will wear me down and that I'll give in and be stupid again.

Ms Black sets her empty glass down just as I'm about to leave. "Thank you again for that," she nods at me. Sinéad and I spent something like half an hour debating whether or not it was acceptable to buy your teachers a drink, and then deliberated over which cocktail to purchase for her.

"Are you off?"

"Some of us still have to go into school tomorrow," she smiles. "Best of luck in the exams, Vicky. You'll sail through them."

This is clearly why it's a great idea to buy drinks for teachers, the little cynical part of my brain says, but I'm practically floating as I rejoin the group.

And then it hits me.

"I have had an epiphany," I announce to Alan, who I've been sticking close to this past while so as to avoid awkwardness with Colm.

"What kind of epiphany?"

"A CAO epiphany. I'm not going to change my list."

"What d'you have down first, arts?"

"Yep. That's what I want to do. I want to do maths and I want to do politics and I want to do sociology and that's the best way of doing it. I want to play around with numbers and go write essays and . . ." I sigh happily. Suddenly it is okay not to know exactly where I want to end up. Because at least I know what I want to do next.

"That's a crap epiphany," he says, but he hugs me anyway.

"Hey, I don't make fun of your epiphanies," I say.

"I have better epiphanies."

"Shut up. Listen, do you want Anna's number or not?"

He looks at me. I look at him, gleeful.

"You think you're so smart," he says, and then pauses. "Yeah, go on, then."

I twirl around the dance floor. Everything's okay, everything's wonderful, everyone's happy and joyful and sparkling . . .

It's only when we're all saying goodbye that I remember. "See you in two weeks," everyone keeps saying. For a second my brain wonders: what's in two weeks? What's happening then?

Ah. Yes. The Leaving Cert. That minor detail. Ah.

34

Anna

"Are you sure you want to come?" Mom asks me for the fifth time in as many minutes. "We'll be seeing lots more of him, there's no hurry."

"I'm sure," I say. "I'll be fine."

Denise's room in the hospital is already filled with balloons and flowers and cards, even though George – nine pounds, two ounces – is less than a day old.

I am used to the newborn babies that they have in medical dramas – the ones that are really a couple of months old – so I am amazed at how tiny he is.

"Isn't he gorgeous?" Denise is glowing.

The whole scandal of it, the unplanned disastrousness of it all, melts away as everyone coos over the baby, all soft voices and ridiculous grins. I couldn't have missed this.

It's early evening by the time we get home. I eat dinner with my parents and then resume the usual pattern. *Macbeth* – no, I know that backwards and forwards at this point. I'll look over my comparative texts instead. Briefly. I'm as ready as I'm going to be, right?

Camomile tea, and then an early night. I try to think about soothing things. Even thinking about James will do. My imaginary version of him, that is.

And then it's morning.

Okay. Here we go.

The school is alive with nervous energy. Good luck is being wished all over the place.

It's really happening. It's really here.

I touch the pink paper reverently. This is ours. Not the mock, not a past paper, but our exam. *Leaving Certificate Examination. English – Higher Level – Paper 1.*

It's like bungee-jumping, opening up that paper. I'm terrified. I'm elated.

I start to write.

By paper two my hand is about ready to fall off. I ramble on about the unseen poem for a bit, then answer the poetry and comparative questions. The expected questions – kingship, role of women – on *Macbeth* don't come up. Instead even the lesser of the two evils is my least favourite kind of question. What relevance does this play have for today's students? What relevance indeed, I think.

My mind goes blank. I know there's a lot of stuff I can say here, several different ways of rephrasing all the points I've learned off so that they suit the question, but I can't access any of that information. I should've looked over my notes yesterday. No, forget that. Concentrate. Do I dare risk arguing that the play has no relevance at all? It'd be an interesting slant, at least. Do I have enough to back me up on that, though?

I was so hoping for a question on Lady Macbeth. I've practically all of her lines memorised.

Mrs Mooney says she's probably the most evil of all of Shakespeare's heroines. She's ruthless. She pushes Macbeth. She –

But he's the really evil one. We just see her as evil because – because –

I look at the clock. I'm really going to be rushing this.

She's a woman. Ambitious men are fine, we expect that of them. Women, on the other hand –

And there I go. I start scribbling.

It'll either pay off, or it really won't. Do they really want me to write what I believe in or would regurgitating something have been a better idea?

I hand up the paper and force myself to put it out

of my mind. I clench and unclench my fist, trying to rid the tension from six hours of writing.

The next morning is maths paper one. For the first time I notice that the instructions are to *attempt six questions.* Not 'do', but 'attempt'. I hope that's not a bad omen.

I breathe in deeply, pick up my pen, and bungee-jump my way in.

35

Vicky

"What sadistic fiend designed this timetable?" I ask Jen as we pick up our bags at the end of the day. It's twenty-five past four. Putting maths paper two and geography on the same day was not a wise move by the exam commission, I feel.

"My hand hurts," she says wearily. "And we're in until five tomorrow."

Tomorrow is French and biology. Written paper, aural, written paper. I can't wait for it all to be over. My last exam isn't until next week, though. Physics, hanging over my head.

"I bet if people looked at the exam timetables before picking their subjects," I say, "we'd end up making completely different choices."

"I would have," she says. "Music. God. What was I thinking?" Music is one of the very last exams. I pat her shoulder in sympathy.

When I get home I open up the newspaper for the bits about the exams. I'm not sure why I do this to myself. The exam diary thing, the annoying brat they have writing a daily report of how he's getting on, makes me want to stab someone. He's just so *reasonable* about the whole thing, talking about how he's getting plenty of exercise in between studying, how he's pretty confident about that Irish paper, how he was pleased to see a particular question come up . . .

When I read his report on Tuesday evening, after I've survived six out of my seven subjects, I scowl. He sounds positively delighted about the mix of 'challenging and straightforward' questions that came up in maths paper two. I thought that all in all it was a pretty decent exam, but I wouldn't say that in a national newspaper. For God's sake. I look at the analysis of the various subjects but they annoy me too. All these teachers saying students 'should have had no trouble' with this or 'would have been well prepared for' that. Like they know how the students felt when they were actually sitting the exam.

It's weird, though, having all this stuff in print about the exams. As though it's news. As though it's important to everyone.

I still feel like I'm waiting for the sixth year exam-oriented part of my brain to kick in, so that I can believe it.

On Monday, I get through the physics paper quickly, read over it, and then raise my hand. I hand over the paper, and walk out.

Okay. Now what?

36

Anna

I finish on the final Tuesday. Chemistry is on in the afternoon, which means I have the entire morning to get nervous. I look over my notes. I check and double-check my bag to make sure I have everything. Calculator, non-programmable. Pens. Bottle of water.

At five past five on Tuesday evening, I step out of the school and walk home in a daze. It's over. There's nothing else I can do, nothing more I can learn off or write down. It's over.

Now what do I do?

Statement of Provisional Results at the Leaving Certificate Examination: Victoria Marie Shaw

Irish	B3
English	A2

Maths	A1
French	B3
Biology	B3
Geography	A2
Physics	A1

Statement of Provisional Results at the Leaving Certificate Examination: Anna Elizabeth Foster

Irish	A1
English	B2
Maths	A2
Biology	A1
French	A2
Chemistry	A1
Accounting	A1

Epilogue

Anna looks at the slip of paper in her hand and tries to have perspective. She thinks she probably should have it at this stage, but that B2 in English might as well be a glowing neon sign on the page, the way it stands out.

A2 in maths, after all that. But her French grade is an unexpected bonus. She has five hundred and eighty points. Not six hundred. She'll get into medicine, she knows, but there's still something empty about the whole thing. She feels a twinge of regret, just what she wanted to avoid.

"Oh, for God's sake," Vicky says, rolling her eyes, "stop staring at it. Five-eighty, we get it, you're brilliant."

Jen's busy counting up her points. "Four hundred and ninety, I think," she says, passing it over to Vicky to check. "What did you get?"

Vicky has yet to add up her own, knowing she's well over what she needs. "Oh, I don't know," she says vaguely, adding up Jen's. "Yeah, four-ninety. Right, what do I have here . . ." She's torn about her own results. Disappointed about biology. Apathetic about her languages. Thrilled about geography. Surprised by English. Pleased with physics and maths, but more relieved than anything else. "Five hundred and thirty," she says. She imagines, for a moment, what her results might have been if she'd worked the way Anna did, if she'd followed through on her good intentions.

Sinéad's just finished calculating her own points. "Five twenty," she announces, then looks at Vicky. "God, you bitch. Some of us actually *worked* last year."

"Oh, shh, you're all total nerds," Jen says.

"Were you talking to Alan?" Vicky asks Anna as they walk down the corridor.

"Yeah. Five-sixty. He's thrilled."

"Everyone's done so well," Vicky marvels. "No disaster stories yet." Not really, she thinks. No disasters, just disappointments.

"Give it time," Anna says, still not entirely convinced that she's not a disaster story.

"Don't be so negative!" Jen says. "We did it! We survived!"

"And now we go out into the real world," Sinéad says, adopting a fake-cheerful tone.

"No, now we go to college," Vicky corrects her.

"Entirely different," Anna agrees.

"Not the real world at all, really," Vicky says.

"I'm not sure the real world even exists," Anna plays along.

"Probably just a vicious rumour."

"Or a giant conspiracy."

"You're on to something there."

The doors of the school swing shut behind them and they laugh, giddily, their way to the gates.